NOW YOU KNOW

BY PHYLLIS KIEFFE

ISBN: 978-0-578-68210-5

Romance is always a mystery.

PROLOGUE

Donna Taylor came from a very wealthy and prominent family. She was in her mid-thirties, very beautiful with long, thick blonde hair and very blue eyes, petite, about 5'4", and very shapely. She was an only child and was a Daddy's girl. Don, her father, adored her and made sure she always had everything she needed or wanted. Her mother had passed away earlier, but had instilled in Donna that it was important to always give back. Donna's father continued to help his daughter honor this commitment, and she worked tirelessly raising money for the underprivileged and doing charity work in the community.

She adored her father, Don. He was extremely wealthy and was a prominent member of the community. He lived in a magnificent estate in Palos Verdes with his loveable boxer dog, Murphy and Henry, his chatty, but somewhat neurotic parrot. He had bought a beautiful new townhome for his daughter which was close by his home in the influential area.

Lieutenant Stephen McClary was in charge of homicide at the LAPD in Southern California. He was in his forties, very dignified looking, tall, about 6'2", and very attractive. He had been in charge of homicide for the past fifteen years and had an outstanding record. He was highly respected by his peers. His top detective team was Ramon Ruiz and his partner, Ted Siciliano.

The lieutenant had been a widower for some time and had met Donna through an investigation of her two prior husband's unexpected deaths. The deaths proved to be accidental with no foul play. David Collins, her first husband died from a heart attack, and her second husband, Dr. Bill Townsend died from an accidental pool drowning at their home. Their deaths were confirmed by forensics and an autopsy report. There had been no foul play.

Donna met her first husband, David Collins through both of their two best friends Sheila and Bob.

David was a knockout. He was single, about 6'4", 210-220lbs, thick black hair, dark eyes and very physically fit. Women were attracted to him like a magnet because of his good looks and charm.

David became the love of Donna's life. With the help of John, his father, David began investing in apartment buildings. David's bank account began to increase steadily with his investments. When they decided to marry, David's father could foresee a political future for his son and his future wife. Donna was very wealthy and from a prominent family, and was known for her contributions to the community. John felt his son was becoming well known for his apartment redevelopment projects in the community. All of this would be a tremendous asset for David's political future.

Donna never realized her husband was a womanizer until she discovered suggestive photos of a woman who looked exactly like her. The two women were what are called "*look-alikes*". The woman's name was Sandy Grant. They both had thick, long blonde hair and very blue eyes. Both were in their mid-thirties, about the same size, 5'4", very petite and shapely. She and Donna had never met and were not related.

Sandy Grant was from a small town in Northern California and was from the opposite side of the social spectrum from Donna. She spent her youth in foster homes until a family she had become close to, the Bowers, rescued her at the age of 16 and she became a part of their family. Sandy excelled in her studies at school and eventually graduated from a small business college there. After graduation, she fell in love with a salesman. They married and decided to move to Southern California. They had always wanted to live close to the water. Unfortunately, he was killed in an automobile accident two years later.

Sandy was devastated by his death. From his insurance benefits, she was able to purchase a small power boat which she could live aboard in a small marina in San Pedro. She always kept in close touch with the Bowers family, especially Alecia, their daughter, and Alecia's son Brian. Alecia and Sandy were like sisters. Alone and very vulnerable at the time after her husband's death, Sandy met David Collins at "The Wharf", a bar and grill close to her boat and they started an affair.

Devastated by David's affair after seeing the revealing photos, Donna divorced him. The divorce caused David's net worth to plummet to a new low.

David blamed Sandy for his divorce, he felt that if it hadn't been for those damn photos Donna, his wife, would have never known the difference.

David's father was the only one who knew he was a womanizer. He warned him repeatedly to be discreet. But this latest fiasco was the last straw. His father was livid. He refused to help him monetarily anymore. He told his son, "I am not a god damn money tree!"

David's philandering left him close to nothing in the divorce settlement and he was in need of cash desperately. He needed to return to the house where he and Donna lived after they were married. He had completely forgotten the watch his father had given him for his college graduation. It was some kind of rare Rolex and very valuable. He had hidden it in the back of one of his desk drawers. He only wore it on special occasions. He didn't see Donna's car in the driveway so he knew she wasn't home. He knew she had all the locks changed, but the side door in the garage was usually left unlocked. He still had the garage door opener in his glove compartment. Maybe that still worked. It did. He drove into the garage, got out, and went to the side door. Holding his breath, he turned the knob. It opened. He hurried into the study and found his Rolex, just where he had left it. Thank goodness it was still there! He grabbed the watch with the case and put it in the pocket of his jacket.

Just as he started to leave, he saw someone standing dangerously close to the edge of the steep cliff on their property. David had planned to put in a retaining wall as a safety precaution but intermittent rains delayed the project. In the interim, he had Danger and No Trespassing signs put in front of the steep drop. Apparently, the Danger and No Trespassing signs were being ignored by someone. Through the thick vegetation he could see blonde hair blowing in the wind. He looked closer. It was Sandy. She must have walked up the backside of the grade. She looked like she was in some kind of trance. David thought, what in the hell is she doing up here? For Christ's sake the woman had ruined his life! David saw his opportunity and took it. He crept up silently behind her and shoved her as hard as he could. Then he stood there and watched her fall all the way down into the ravine below. He returned to his car, got in, and made a clean getaway. His recently rented electric car moved quietly down the long steep driveway, the engine only making the sound of a light wind. Smiling, he felt much better. It had been a good day after all.

Sandy's body was found in the ravine shortly afterwards. It looked like she had fallen from the steep cliff on Donna and David's property in Palos Verdes. Foul play was definitely suspected and the case was under investigation.

Sandy was mistakenly pronounced dead and taken to the medical examiner's office. When the ME discovered she was still alive, but only barely, they attached life support equipment and rushed her to the ER at USC Medical Center. Sandy went through months and months of painful operations and plastic surgeries. Miraculously, she survived and the doctors successfully put her back together again. She and David's wife, Donna were no longer look-alikes, but Sandy was just as beautiful as ever.

When Sandy was fully recovered after months and months

of painful surgeries she was released from the hospital. Her case was still under investigation. Foul play was definitely suspected. Eventually she started to recover slowly on her own. Lieutenant Stephen McClary took her under his wing to keep an eye on her. He found her a very nice downstairs apartment owned by a friend of his which was perfect for her recovery.

Feeling more like herself every day, Sandy decided to venture outside and go on a little shopping spree. Maybe even a nice lunch by the ocean at Breaker's 9. Just as she was finishing her lunch at the Breaker's, she recognized a voice behind her.

"May I join you and buy you a drink?"

A cold chill ran down her spine. It was David.

"Why yes, you can."

She didn't know why she agreed, but she did.

When they introduced themselves, she gave him a false name. David thought she was so beautiful and of course had no idea who she really was. He thought it was his lucky day. He ordered drinks for them and they made small talk. Afterwards, he suggested that she follow him in her car to his apartment for another drink so they could become better acquainted. She agreed. That was why David loved the Breaker's. It was a great pick-up place.

While at his apartment, she drugged his drink without him knowing with some of her strong pain pills. When he was in a weakened stupor from the pills, she identified herself.

"You don't recognize me, do you? My name is SANDY GRANT!!"

She could see the panic in his eyes just before he passed out.

She didn't feel the drugs would kill him, but it just made her feel good to have the upper hand. She wanted him to see that she had survived that horrible fall. So *now you know.*

Deep down inside she always felt that it was David who had pushed her down that steep cliff. She needed some kind of vindication. Maybe that's why she went to his apartment.

David never recovered from his unconscious state. He died of a natural heart attack. Forensics determined that the drugs in his drink were not strong enough to cause his death.

But this is what the authorities didn't know. They had no indication that Sandy was in his apartment and when she identified herself to David as Sandy Grant, the shock alone could have caused him to have a major heart attack, but *now you know*. Later, after David's death, circumstantial evidence proved that David was the guilty party who had pushed Sandy down the steep cliff. The case was finally closed, but no one ever knew what really happened when David returned to retrieve his Rolex watch and actually pushed Sandy down the steep cliff. Not even the authorities, but *now you know*.

Donna's second marriage was to a Dr. Bill Townsend, a psychiatrist. She was devastated from the divorce of her first marriage to David. She went to see a professional, Dr. Townsend, for help. She was close to a nervous breakdown and she became infatuated with Bill. He eventually convinced her to marry him. She had no idea he was a predator of wealthy women. The marriage lasted only two and a half months after he quit his job and became an alcoholic. He became mentally abusive to her and he began to threaten her. She became terrified of him and knew he had a gun. Her attorney had the marriage annulled and placed a restraining order on him.

Bill was also a suspect in the fall of Sandy Grant. He didn't know her, but because she and his ex-wife were look-alikes, he might have thought it was Donna standing on that steep cliff instead of Sandy.

The doctor was enraged because he received nothing of monetary value after the marriage was annulled. Donna came home late one night and saw the security lights had been breached over the pool. She could see something large by the side of the pool. Oh my god, it was Bill! He had fallen over some debris by the pool and was unconscious. She could see a gun handle protruding from his coat pocket. Panicking, she thought how much longer can this go on before he finally kills me? He had even tried to have her killed after the annulment. Thank goodness it was unsuccessful. She knew he would keep trying until he succeeded, and he would get away with it. Donna wasn't going to wait for that to happen. She grabbed the skimmer net by the pool and placed the pole side against his back and gave a little nudge. He slid gracefully into the pool and drowned. In her panicked state, she called Lieutenant McClary. He was on his way home and close by. After the lieutenant, 911, and forensics had completed their investigations, they ruled Bill's death as a drowning accident. But *now you know* what really happened. Donna always felt her actions were justified.

CHAPTER 1

Donna and Lieutenant Stephen McClary, head of the Los Angeles Police Department homicide division, were returning home after just being married in Catalina. They spent three days enjoying everything from water sports for Stephen and shopping for treasures for Donna. They were on the Catalina Express vessel and would arrive at its San Pedro terminal in about forty-five minutes.

"Stephen, I keep forgetting to ask you, why didn't you go on the zip line?"

Stephen thought about it.

"Too many donuts."

"What does that mean? Was there a weight restriction of some kind?"

"Yeah, I think I was okay, but I didn't want to frighten any of the other zip liners."

"Maybe you better cut down on those donuts, Stephen. I can pack you a healthy lunch every day, full of nice green vegetables."

"Donna, if you do that, I won't be able to do my job."

"For crying out loud Stephen, what do those donuts do for you?"

"They make me think."

"Stephen, that makes no sense whatsoever."

"Trust me on this, Donna. They are an important part of my daily routine. You know I have a lot of stress at work."

"For Pete's sake, don't I help relieve your stress?"

"More than you know sweetheart, but that's just in the evening."

"Well, let's discuss your donut addiction another time."

Stephen had his arm around Donna and she snuggled into him.

"Tell me Mrs. McClary, did you enjoy yourself with me during this time?"

"Of course, I did."

Even when Donna was previously married before Stephen, she always made it a point to go to Catalina by herself. It was a girl thing. She just enjoyed going by herself to shop and do her thing.

"What did you like most about having me along?"

"Well Stephen, during the day we both did whatever we wanted."

"How about the evenings?"

"Well, I loved our romantic evenings. Dining and drinking by candlelight at all the fine restaurants."

"Anything else?"

"Yes, going back to our hotel afterwards and hitting the sheets. You finally got that out of me, didn't you?"

"You know you're a relentless tease."

"I know," she said.

Stephen held her closer and whispered in her ear,

"But that's one of the many things I love about you."

He started to say something else, but she was fast asleep with a smile on her face. Stephen was so glad they were finally married. She had two previous marriages which turned into disasters.

Donna finally had her life back after her two previous divorces, and she wanted to keep it that way. She and Stephen were very much in love, and she was very content to keep their relationship just the way it was without getting married. However, Stephen, a widower, was a firm believer of marriage and finally convinced her, but it took some doing.

They had told no one they were getting married, except her

father. They wanted to surprise their closest friends when they returned home. They planned to have an early holiday dinner before Christmas at her father's home and surprise everyone with their announcement before Stephen returned to work.

Donna had had good luck shopping at one of her favorite stores in Catalina that specialized in beautiful handmade tiles. She always loved everything she purchased in Catalina, but she could never have enough of the tiles. Her other favorite store had a number of unusual masks that were actually made in Indonesia. She had purchased a large number of very unusual ones.

"I can hardly wait to get home, Stephen and unpack all these things so you can see what I bought. You know Stephen, we should bring in the New Year in Catalina with a few of our good friends. Let's remember to do that and make a reservation in time at the casino for their special New Year's party."

After they were married in Catalina, Stephen and Donna celebrated and had a nice lunch overlooking the water. Afterwards, they checked in at their hotel and decided how to spend the rest of the day. Donna could hardly wait to go shopping and did so. The minute she left Stephen was on his cell phone. It had beeped right as they were getting ready to board the Catalina Express to leave for Catalina. Stephen promised Donna he would not answer his phone while they were away, but the minute he was alone, Stephen pushed the button. It was his ace detective.

"Hi lieutenant, this is Ramon." Just letting you know about a serial assailant traveling through Southern California, robbing and assaulting women. I just wanted to let you know in case you heard something about it on the news. Looks like he might be heading this way. I didn't want you to worry. Ted and I are on it. Have a good time."

He would make this his first priority the first day he returned to work.

CHAPTER 2

Raymond Martin had never worked a day in his life. He didn't have to. He made a living by taking other people's money. He liked to rob and assault unsuspecting women. He would follow them as they left a shopping center, to where they lived.

He had planned to leave Arizona for California right away. He couldn't stand another summer in that sweltering heat and was looking forward to cooler weather. But his plans were put temporarily on hold. Late one night a hit and run driver totaled his car outside his apartment. He couldn't afford another car.

He had to think of something. And then he had an idea. He knew his idea carried much more serious consequences than any of his previous crimes. But he was smart and he had managed so far not to get caught. He had no criminal record of any kind. How many could say that?! Not many, that's for sure. He bought an Arizona Sunday paper and started reading the classifieds for automobiles for sale. One ad caught his eye. It read, "Like new, Lexus for sale by owner."

He called the telephone number given.

"Hello."

"I saw your ad in the paper for the Lexus and am very interested."

"You're welcome to come by and take a look." The owner gave him his address, "I will be home all morning."

Raymond thought, perfect. The owner's address was close by.

"I can be there in an hour."

"That would be fine."

Raymond called a cab on his throw away phone. He had the driver drop him off a block from the owner's home. Raymond rang the doorbell at 10:30 am. He introduced himself and showed the owner his driver's license. The Lexus was sitting in the driveway.

Raymond asked him, "Why are you selling your car?"

"I am a recent widower and I don't need two cars. My other one is in the garage." He took the car keys out of his pocket and said, "Would you like to drive it?"

"Yes, I would."

Raymond removed his gun from his pocket and shot the owner point blank.

The owner never knew what hit him. Raymond thought that if any of the neighbors were home and heard the shot, they would probably think a car had backfired. People didn't seem to react to anything out of the ordinary like they used to.

Raymond drove the Lexus back to his apartment and picked up a large suitcase with all his belongings. He left a note for the owner at his apartment. He said he was sorry, but he had an emergency and had to give up the apartment. Raymond got back in the Lexus and drove away very carefully, obeying all traffic rules. In about two hours, he reached a small city in California. He spotted a rundown car dealership with surprisingly quite a few cars for sale. He would come back in the morning when they opened. He took the Lexus to a nearby car wash and had it thoroughly cleaned inside and out. He put on his driving gloves and would keep them on whenever he was in or out of the Lexus.

When he came to a nearby motel which had a restaurant, he decided to stay there that night. He asked the owner if there was a shopping center nearby. There was and he drove to the center later that night. He needed to dump the Arizona license plates on the Lexus right away. He parked in an obscure corner of the mall, removed a California plate from a parked car and put it on the Lexus. He dumped the Arizona plates in a dumpster on his way back to the motel. Before turning in, Raymond parked the Lexus in back of his motel room and cleaned the inside again.

After a good night's sleep and a big breakfast in the morning, Raymond headed back to the car dealership he had noticed earlier. The minute Raymond drove into the dealership, a man came out of his office to greet him.

"Hi there, I'm Ben Harper, the owner. How may I help you?" Raymond introduced himself.

"I would like to trade my Lexus for a smaller, medium-priced car." Right away he could see the owner loved the Lexus.

"Let me show you some of my best models, Mr. Martin."

Raymond saw one he liked. They negotiated and made a trade. The owner gave him a decent amount of cash for the remaining balance, no questions asked.

When he left the dealership with his trade, Raymond felt good. He had a relatively new medium-priced car with a valid California license plate, plus a good amount of cash in his pocket. Not bad for a day's work and for Ben Harper too, the dealership owner. He had a beautiful Lexus luxury car almost like new which he had always wanted.

CHAPTER 3

After Donna and Stephen arrived home from Catalina and were enjoying a drink in the den, Donna said,

"When do you think we should have our surprise party to announce our marriage?"

"Well, I still have a few days before I return to work. How about the first Saturday night before I return to work?"

"Okay, that sounds good. I was thinking of having it at my father's. What do you think?" Donna's father lived in the Estates area of Palos Verdes, close to their townhouse.

"Sounds perfect. Your father loves to entertain at his place and show off Murphy and Henry. You know how they love to provide the entertainment for everyone."

Murphy was her father's boxer dog who loved showing off, and Henry was his neurotic parrot.

"I'll send out the invitations saying it's an early holiday dinner party. Of course, I intend to have everything catered."

Donna never cooked anything if she could help it. She always called her special caterer, Andre who prepared everything and even had it delivered in Donna's serving dishes that he always kept on hand for her.

CHAPTER 4

"I was thinking of inviting only our closest friends. That would keep the guests to no more than ten. Is that okay with you, Stephen?"

"Sounds good to me."

"Let's see, we have Connie, my dad's personal friend for sure, I think they're becoming more than just bridge partners, what do you think Stephen?"

"I agree."

"Remember the night we were at Dominic's? Who did we see sitting across the room from us having a romantic dinner? None other than my dad and Connie. You even sent them over a bottle of my dad's favorite red wine. He loved that. They waved back at us and I think my dad was a little embarrassed and was even blushing a little."

"I remember, yes."

"Then, there is your ace detective Ramon and his beautiful wife, Sandy, even though we are no longer "*look a-likes*" after her fall." Even though Sandy was one of the many women Donna's first husband, David, had an affair with Donna no longer held any resentment towards her. In fact, she and Donna had recently become very close friends.

Lieutenant McClary considered Ramon the best detective he had ever had. His Latino good looks also made him the best-looking detective in the department, and needless to say, the most popular with all the females working there. He had been single for a long time until Sandy. Ramon met Sandy through the lieutenant while she was recovering from her fall. Ramon fell hard and his single life came abruptly to an end. They fell in love and were married shortly thereafter.

"Then my best friends Sheila and Bob."

Donna had been classmates with them at the University of Southern California (USC) and they had all remained best of friends after graduation. They had introduced her to David, also a USC classmate and friend. Sheila did fund raising and charity work the same as Donna; and her husband, Bob, had a successful CPA practice. They enjoyed going out with Donna and Stephen and attending the same benefits and parties.

"Next, there's Ted and Janet. Your other best detective, and his wife."

Ted and Ramon had been partners for five years. They had the highest number of closed cases in the homicide department. Ted was very proud of his Italian heritage and he and Janet had given an Italian purebred kitty to Sandy and Ramon as a wedding present. Appropriately, her Italian name was Angelina.

"Last but certainly not least is Ivan. He may or may not bring a date."

"Stephen, I don't know what we would do without Ivan. He is the best thing that ever happened to us."

"Without a doubt, Donna."

"That's all I can think of Stephen. Can you think of anyone I left out?"

"I think you've got it covered, hon."

CHAPTER 5

Right after Donna's divorce from David, the tenants in her apartments became unbearable, causing her all kinds of trouble. They knew that David no longer managed the apartments and took advantage of the situation. Donna was solely responsible for the property management. A friend had referred her to someone he knew that could help her. His name was Ivan. When Donna first met Ivan, she knew her friend had referred her to the right person. He was huge, 6'4" about 220lbs and very muscular and strong looking. His transportation was a big black Harley. Lots of thick black hair covered his head and he dressed in black from his big black leather jacket down to his big black boots. A gold earring decorated one ear and he had a shiny gold tooth right in front that glistened if he ever smiled. Ivan made a very scary statement indeed.

Ivan did a beautiful job of turning Donna's apartments around. He got rid of the riff raff tenants, renovated the apartments inside and outside with a fresh coat of paint. He increased the rents to what they should be and filled them with qualified tenants. Donna now had a positive cash flow and no vacancies.

Ivan became known to Donna as "Ivan the Enforcer". She

turned the property management over to him for all five of her apartment buildings.

Ivan was also the leader of a biker group of about twenty men. The group had an excellent reputation for helping the community with any work they needed to have done. The projects could range from small handyman tasks to larger, more complicated ones. They were well qualified, honest, dependable and of course they charged far less than other contractors. Because the men were massive and strong, ranging from 6'2" to 6'5", 200 to 300lbs they could do projects that the average man could not do. By serving the community, they were also able to make a pretty good living for themselves. Ivan also had an eye for keeping the community safe. He had helped Lieutenant McClary solve so many cases in his department that it was becoming embarrassing. The lieutenant would love to hire Ivan permanently in his homicide department but he knew his wife, Donna, would never forgive him and he would never hear the end of it.

CHAPTER 6

Donna had checked with her father, Don earlier to make sure it was okay to have the party at his place. He was delighted.

"I'll be sure to let Murphy and Henry know, so they have enough time to rehearse."

Donna laughed, "Oh Dad, don't be so silly."

"Well you have to admit Murphy and Henry are a bit unusual and they certainly are a lot more entertaining than your last two husbands."

"You have a point, Dad. I bet they are enjoying being together all the time at your house, aren't they?"

"They're loving it and keeping me younger with all their crazy antics."

Henry, the parrot, used to be at Donna's house. Her father had given Henry to his daughter after her two bad marriages. He thought she needed better company. But Henry and Murphy missed each other so much, Donna gave Henry back to her father to be with Murphy. Everyone was much happier and Henry's language had improved immensely. When he was at Donna's, Henry had picked up the sexual innuendos from Donna and Stephen's lovemaking and liked to mimic them. This got to be extremely embarrassing whenever they had company.

CHAPTER 7

Raymond continued his robbing and assaulting spree as he drove through the cities, toward the ocean. He would always pick a well-dressed woman with a nice car. He would follow her to her residence, knock on her door or ring the doorbell. If she looked though a peephole or a window, she would see a clean-cut, nicely dressed man. Nine times out of ten she would open the door. The minute she opened the door he would plant his foot in the doorway and be inside in the blink of an eye. He would take whatever cash she had, assault her if necessary, and threaten her enough so she would make a very poor witness.

Recently he had added two rapes to his M.O. He would never rob more than one woman in the same city. He simply would drive on to another city and choose another victim. He felt this would not raise as much attention with the local authorities. So far, he had no criminal record.

Raymond continued driving more towards the ocean. He always liked being close to the water. By the time he reached some of the waterfront cities, Raymond had successfully forced himself into four residences in four different cities. When Raymond came to the beach cities close to the water he fell in love with the city of San Pedro.

Raymond liked everything about it. Maybe he might want to stay there for a while. He found a cheap but relatively clean motel.

The next morning, he asked the motel owner, "Could you recommend a good restaurant for breakfast?"

"I sure can. Curly's Bar and Grill. It's right across the street from the Post Office downtown. Not only is it good, but it's the best anywhere."

He gave Raymond directions. Raymond thanked him, "I'll give it a try."

"You won't be sorry." Said the owner.

CHAPTER 8

Darlene, was the customer's favorite server at Curly's Bar and Grill. She was in her early forties. Her bright red hair was piled high on her head in an old-fashioned beehive style accentuated with bright yellow ribbons. She wore a tight black uniform which displayed a lot of her ample cleavage.

Darlene missed going out with Ivan, but they both knew it was an impossible relationship. She just wasn't the biker type and he understood that. His Harley Davidson was an extension of his life, but she was glad they remained very good friends. Ivan loved to tease her.

"You know, Darlene, even though you're not a biker, you know what they say?"

"What, Ivan?"

"Nobody's perfect."

Ivan came into Curly's on a regular basis and Darlene would join him if she wasn't too busy just to catch up on things. There was usually a steady stream of customers, mostly male, because the food portions were large, delicious, reasonably priced, and you couldn't beat the service you got from Darlene.

One morning, a new fellow came in which Darlene had not seen before. He was about her age, early forties and average looking. She introduced herself, snapping her gum.

"Hi there, I'm Darlene, your server, what would you like? Coffee or something to drink to start with?"

"Coffee sounds great."

Darlene took him his coffee.

"Boy, I need this."

"I don't think I've seen you in here before. Are you new in town?"

"Pretty new, my name is Ray. It's nice to meet you, Darlene. I'll have the steak, medium rare, scrambled eggs, hash browns, and toast."

"Good choice, Ray."

Darlene hustled off to put in his order.

When Ray was leaving, he said, "See you again soon, Darlene. The food was great and so was the service."

He left her a very generous tip.

CHAPTER 9

Ivan came into Curly's the next morning before going to work. He sat down in his regular booth.

"Good morning, Darlene. I'll have my usual. When you have a moment, could you join me for a minute?"

"Sure, big guy."

Darlene sat down across from him, "Okay, what's up?"

"Have you seen the warning on TV about the robber/assault guy?"

"Yes, I have."

"Have you noticed anyone new that's come into Curly's?"

"Yes, as a matter of fact, a guy about my age came in yesterday morning, said his name was Ray."

"When he comes in again, I want you to point him out to me."

"Well Ivan, you're in luck. He just walked in the door and has on a green plaid shirt. You can't miss him."

"Will you do me a big favor, Darlene?"

"Probably."

"When Ray leaves, put his tray in the back. Pick up his water glass with a clean napkin, carefully. Make sure not to touch it, and throw out any water in the glass. Place the glass in a clean take-out bag for me. I'll be back in a little while and pick it up."

"This is exciting Ivan, just like those detective shows on TV."

"Thank you for helping Darlene."

Ivan was always on high alert for any ongoing community problems. That was why Lieutenant McClary considered him his best non-official detective.

When Ivan left Curly's, he removed his camera from his backpack on his bike and walked across the street to the busy post office facing Curly's. Ivan waited until he saw Ray leave Curly's, then snapped his picture. When Ray went to his car, Ivan was also able to get a good shot of his car and license plate. Ivan got on his bike and followed Ray at a safe distance when he drove off. Ivan was curious and wanted to see where he was staying. It was a cheap motel, not far away. Ray parked his car in front of his room and went inside. There was a little shopping area across the street from the motel. Ivan parked his bike there and found a comfortable place to sit where he could keep an eye on Ray's car and not be seen. Ivan called his friend, the lieutenant on his cell phone and explained.

"Lieutenant, this is Ivan. I hope I'm not overreacting, but I have an uneasy feeling about a new guy in town."

Ivan had an impeccable reputation with the lieutenant and his department. He had helped them solve more crimes than they could count.

"You know I trust your judgement, Ivan. Tell me your concerns."

"Can you have someone run this guy's license plate for me?"

Ivan gave him his license plate number.

"Sure, I'll call you back in a few minutes."

The lieutenant called back shortly.

"Ivan nothing unusual on the license plate, but let's don't count this guy out yet. I trust your instincts."

"You're the boss, lieutenant. Also, lieutenant, I know this may seem a little premature, but I also have a water glass with his DNA. I'll drop it off at the station for you. Just in case we need it if we think he may be involved in the current robbery/assaults. Just to be on the safe side."

"What would I do without you, Ivan. You're always a step ahead of us."

"Thank you, lieutenant, all in a day's work."

CHAPTER 10

Ivan had breakfast at Curly's every morning before he went to work. Darlene, the server, always took his order. He missed going out with her. They had stopped dating because Darlene did not like to ride on bikes, period. As he was waiting for his breakfast something occurred to him.

"Darlene, when you have a minute, I want to ask you something."

"Sure, big guy. Give me a minute."

She came back and sat down across from him.

"Now what do you want to ask me?"

"Darlene, my best friends, Donna and the lieutenant are having an early holiday dinner party next Saturday. I would like you to go with me. I have reserved our biker company car for the occasion, hoping you would say yes. They only invited their closest friends, about ten of us. You will know everybody there. Donna wants to have it at her father, Don's house and you know him too."

"It sounds like fun, Ivan. I would love to go with you. What time will you pick me up."

"6:30 sharp."

"I'll be ready. Dressy night?"

"You bet."

Ivan squeezed her hand.

"I can hardly wait Darlene."

"Me too."

"Darlene, I want to apologize again for being so thoughtless. It never occurred to me that you wouldn't like bike riding."

"Well Ivan, I'm pretty fussy about my hair and that damn helmet smashes it down flat."

"Darlene, is your hair your only concern when you ride on my bike?"

"I think so. Why?"

"Well, I was thinking I might be able to get a helmet for you designed like a top hat so your hair wouldn't get flat."

"That's a unique idea, Ivan. Let me think about it."

"Just a thought, Darlene."

"You know Ivan, if that damn man-bun of yours gets any bigger we may have to get a top hat for you, too. Who knows, we might become known as the 'Two Tops'."

Ivan burst out laughing.

"Touché, Darlene."

"On that note Ivan, I better get your breakfast. I think it's ready."

And she sashayed off to the kitchen.

CHAPTER 11

The first Saturday in December came quickly. The minute Don's doorbell rang pandemonium broke out. Murphy made a beeline to the front door to greet whoever was there. Don was right behind him. Henry began shouting,

"Come in. Come in!"

Don greeted everyone with an, "Early happy holidays."

Introductions were not needed. Everyone knew everyone.

"Make yourselves comfortable in the library. You all know where that is. Donna and Stephen are there and will fix drinks for you at the bar."

"I see the rest of our guests are coming up the driveway. We'll join you in the library in a few minutes."

As the remaining guests entered the library, Donna said, "Stephen, look who just came in."

"Oh my god. Is that who I think it is?"

"They make a handsome couple don't they Stephen?"

"They sure do."

It was Ivan and his date, Darlene, from Curley's Bar & Grill.

They were dressed to the nines. Ivan was wearing a stylish men's black suit with a black cashmere turtleneck and a black and gold silk handkerchief was tucked in the suit's breast pocket. He was also wearing very expensive looking men's black shoes. His only jewelry was one gold earring. Darlene was a knockout in a long black dress with a beautifully sequined top. Her hair was swept up in a very attractive French twist dotted with just enough sparkles. Needless to say, they were a big hit with everyone.

CHAPTER 12

Everyone was making a fuss over Murphy and Henry. Henry started muttering to himself on his perch anxious for the fun to begin. Murphy and Henry seemed to know when they had a captive audience. In a loud voice, Don said, "Okay everybody, it's showtime!"

Murphy started the entertainment and grabbed one of his favorite toys, tossed it high in the air and then caught it squeaking it loudly non-stop. On cue, Henry shrieked. Then Murphy went into his spins and Henry went into hysterics. Henry would get so carried away he would sometimes fall off his perch in hysterics. He continued laughing non-stop. This act went on for about fifteen minutes until Don yelled,

"Okay kids that's enough for now. Here's a special treat for each of you," and they finally settled down. Everyone loved Murphy and Henry's performance and broke into applause.

Don said, "Dinner is ready, please be seated."

No one, except Donna's father Don, suspected Donna and Stephen had gotten married. Everyone thought the dinner party was to celebrate the coming Christmas holidays. They all sat down in their respective places at the table. Don was at one end of the table and Stephen at the other with Donna seated next to him. Champagne was served in everyone's glass.

Stephen stood and said, "I would like to make a very special announcement. Donna and I just returned from a three-day vacation in Catalina, where we were married! We are now happily man and wife and we wanted you all to be the first to know."

Everyone stood and cheered, chanting, "Here, here!" and raised their glasses in a toast to the happy bride and groom. The party was a huge success. Everyone had been completely surprised by the marriage announcement. All the guests stayed late, which is always a sign of a very successful party. Last to leave were Ivan and Darlene and Donna and Stephen.

When Donna and Stephen left, she said, "Did you notice Stephen, that Connie didn't leave with the rest of us?"

"I did. She's probably going to help your father clean up after the party or something."

"Or something is right. My father does seem very happy, doesn't he, Stephen?"

"Yes, he does."

"I like her."

"Me too, hon. She seems very nice. They make a very nice couple."

CHAPTER 13

Don and Connie met each other through friends at a party. They discovered they both liked to play bridge and joined a bridge group which played twice a week. They were both widowers and enjoyed each other's company immensely. Connie lived within walking distance of Don's estate. She loved to cook and was an excellent one and enjoyed having Don over for dinner. Her specialties were out of this world. They discovered they had a lot in common and also loved to go out to fine restaurants for dinner on a regular basis. They also took in plays and movies they liked. Both had been happily married but neither was interested in marrying again especially at their age. So far, they had no desire to become more serious. Both led very active lives. They were happy to enjoy each other's company especially someone of the opposite sex without any serious commitment and just have a good time. They had a great relationship and so far, were keeping it status quo.

Both Don and Connie loved to party and were night owls. Sometimes it was too inconvenient for Don to take Connie home when it was really late, even though she lived close by. Don had a guest room with twin beds and at first, he gave Connie one of his pajama tops so she could stay over. He slept in the other twin bed in case she needed anything during the night. Later, she kept a change of clothing in one of his closets.

Connie also loved Murphy and Henry like they were her own. She loved to play games with them.

CHAPTER 14

As Ivan and Darlene were driving back to Darlene's apartment, they were discussing Donna and Stephen's surprise marriage party.

"That was a great party, wasn't it, Darlene?"

"It sure was."

"I noticed all the guys were looking at you, Darlene."

"And all the gals were eying you, Ivan."

"I am so glad Donna and the lieutenant got married. She finally got herself a really nice guy. They are perfect for one another."

"I agree."

"You look so beautiful, Darlene. I hope you are going to ask me to stay over."

"I just might do that, Ivan."

As they entered her apartment, Darlene said, "Ivan, make yourself comfortable. I'm going to make us a couple of after dinner drinks. How does that sound?"

"Great, can I help?"

"No, just make yourself comfortable."

She brought the drinks out and set them on the table in front of the sofa.

"I think you're going to like this."

"That's really good. Darlene, do you think the reason we like each other so much is because we are such good friends?"

"Could be, Ivan. Could be."

Ivan put his drink down and reached for Darlene. They became more intimate, and he began fondling her breasts then his hand moved downward between her legs. Darlene gave a low moan. She could feel his hardness pressing against her leg.

"Ivan, maybe we should go into the bedroom."

When he stood up his pants were bulging.

"Here, let me help get you out of those."

Darlene helped him remove his pants and led him into the bedroom and, not by his hand. They started to remove the rest of their clothing quickly.

Darlene laughed, "Let's be careful with these clothes. They cost a bundle."

"But it was worth it, Darlene."

They fell naked onto the bed.

"Ivan, I want you now."

He didn't waste any time and he entered her deeply. They started moving rhythmically together. Their movement growing faster and faster.

"Oh my god, Ivan, don't stop."

Darlene was losing control. One orgasm coming after another. They both cried out and came to an explosive climax. Exhausted, they fell back on the bed.

"Darlene, why did we wait so long to do this?"

"I'm blaming you, Ivan. You're too busy working all the time."

"Believe me, I am going to cut back."

When they got their second wind, Ivan pulled Darlene on top of him.

"You want me to do all the work now don't you. Okay, well here goes."

She straddled him and he entered her. She started moving in and out riding him faster and faster. They both started to lose control. In the throes of passion, they climaxed together. Exhausted they lay back again to get their breath.

"Darlene, when are we going to do this again? I don't want to wait too long."

"How does this Friday night sound? We both don't have to work on Saturday."

"I'll take you to a nice dinner before we are too tired to go anyplace."

Darlene laughed,

"Sounds good big guy."

"Let's take a shower together, Ivan."

The warm water felt wonderful, and they had fun showering the suds off each other.

"Darlene, I think you wore me out. I'm a little bit shaky."

"Oh, for Pete's sake, Ivan. You are as strong as an ox."

"But I haven't had that kind of exercise for quite a while, maybe since the last time we were together."

Ivan and Darlene always had a thing for one another, but Ivan always had too many projects going on to really make it work.

"Well, you better get yourself in shape, Ivan, because you've got me spoiled now."

CHAPTER 15

On his first day back at work from his three-day Catalina marriage vacation, Stephen was enjoying a little peace and quiet in his office. He knew this wouldn't last long. His thoughtful secretary had fresh donuts and coffee waiting for him on his desk. What could be better? He wondered why donuts were always so satisfying. He could certainly eat more than just one, but he noticed all his clothes were getting a little tighter. But what the heck, he deserved another donut after all the mayhem a couple of weeks ago with the capture of the drug gang in San Pedro.

All of a sudden, the silence was interrupted by his office machine spewing out up-to-date information about the robbery/assault problem that Ramon had put on his cell phone when he and Donna were leaving for Catalina. He knew it was too quiet to be true. He got up and read it.

A white male was still on the loose, making his way across Southern California cities preying on women, robbing them of cash, assaulting them and in some cases even raping them. There had been four victims in the last four months and one rape. All of the victims identified him as a white male, average height and weight with no distinguishing marks or features. Not much to go on. None of the victims could give a facial description or wouldn't.

The lieutenant enlarged a map of the area the assailant had covered for his detective's Monday morning meeting. He pinpointed in red the locations the assailant had victimized. It looked like he never picked more than one victim in the same city. He seemed to start at the edge of southern Arizona and move into Southern California making his way towards the ocean. The lieutenant took the bulletin to their weekly 9 am open case meeting. Everyone was brought up-to-date on the robbery/assault case.

A warning would be released on television soon as a reminder for women to keep their premises secure.

"Familiarize yourself with this case. It looks like this guy may be moving into our jurisdiction soon."

Television released the following warning:

Be sure to keep your doors locked and do not open them for anyone unless you are positively sure you know them.

A number was given to call for any questions. It was not necessary to leave your name, only an approximate location.

When Donna, the lieutenant's wife saw the television warning, she called her property manager, Ivan, immediately. The ever-vigilant Ivan told Donna he had already made up a flyer and was sending it to all of the tenants in her buildings.

"Ivan, this guy has me worried. You know, my husband, Stephen thinks you are the best detective ever. Could you let your biker buddies know about this, too?"

"They are already on high alert, Donna."

"Thank you, Ivan." She always felt so much better after talking to him.

The lieutenant had no sooner returned to his office from his staff meeting when he got a call from Ivan about Mr. Robbins. The old adage, 'Time waits for no one' went through the lieutenant's mind. He liked to alter the phrase from "Time" waits for no one to "Crime". It seemed to fit in better with his line of work.

CHAPTER 16

Mr. Robbins was a tenant in one of Donna's apartments. He had been instrumental in the capture of a major drug gang in a San Pedro a couple of weeks ago and was one of the honorees to be honored for his bravery at a special public ceremony. It turned out that the apartment next door to Mr. Robbins was occupied by gang members along with their drug merchandise. Their drugs had been stored in a warehouse close by which had been condemned and they had to move their merchandise out quickly. One of their members suggested they move everything into his apartment temporarily until they found a permanent location. When Mr. Robbins' heard their excessive comings and goings at all hours, he alerted the authorities. Thanks to Mr. Robbins' immediate action, the gang was captured in a major shootout and incarcerated.

A large public ceremony was held in San Pedro to honor everyone responsible for their capture, except Mr. Robbins. Mr. Robbins was the only honoree not to attend the ceremony. It wouldn't take long for someone to figure out Mr. Robbins' might have been the one to blow the whistle on the gang's activities in the apartment.

About a week after the ceremony, Mr. Robbins was home alone reading when his doorbell rang late at night, about 10:30 pm. He wasn't expecting anyone. He decided to pretend he wasn't home. Someone rang his doorbell a few times and then left, when no one answered. Mr. Robbins had also received several hang-up phone calls lately which was unusual. He decided to call Ivan, the property manager. He was always helpful.

"Hi Ivan, this is Mr. Robbins. Sorry to call so late."

"That's okay Mr. Robbins, is anything wrong?"

He told Ivan about what had happened and also about the hang-up phone calls.

"I'm glad you called me, Mr. Robbins. I will look into this and let Lieutenant McClary know. If any of that happens again, please let me know right away."

"Thank you, Ivan."

"You're welcome, Mr. Robbins. I'm glad you called."

Ivan was very concerned about this and called the lieutenant immediately. He told him what had happened.

"I agree with you Ivan. This doesn't sound good."

He and Ivan had been worried that something like this might happen to Mr. Robbins after the ceremony.

"Lieutenant, I'm going to assign one of my bikers, Tiny, to keep an eye on Mr. Robbins for a while. Especially if he leaves his apartment."

"Sounds like a good idea Ivan, we can also patrol the area on a regular basis until this quiets down."

Ivan called Tiny, and told him what he needed to do.

"Just to be on the safe side Tiny, you better carry a piece. These are nasty dudes and they don't mess around."

Tiny was anything but tiny. He was probably the largest of all of Ivan's bikers. Ivan called Mr. Robbins back.

"Mr. Robbins, I have assigned one of my bikers, Tiny, to you. He will be close by if you go out. The lieutenant will also have a patrol car checking your area on a regular basis. If you are planning to go out, call this number. It will alert my biker that you are going out."

"I do need to do a little shopping for groceries tomorrow."

"I'll alert Tiny for you now, Mr. Robbins."

"Thank you, Ivan."

Mr. Robbins opened his door carefully the next day. The hallway was empty so he took the elevator down to go shopping. When he was outside on the street, someone grabbed him roughly and pushed him roughly into the back alley of the apartment.

"You should mind your own business, Mr. Robbins. Why did you alert the authorities about us?"

"I don't know what you are talking about."

The attacker drew out a long stiletto knife.

"Maybe this will help refresh your memory, Mr. Robbins."

Suddenly massive hands wrapped around the attacker's torso and slammed him face first into the concrete wall behind the apartment building. His nose was broken instantly and started bleeding profusely. His face was a bloody mess. When he fell to the ground, his stiletto clattered to the ground next to him. He put out his hand to reach for it and Tiny placed his enormous boot on his hand, crushing it and snapping his fingers like twigs. The attacker screamed in pain.

Tiny said, "This is your last and only warning, asshole. If we see you or any of your kind in this area again you will become a permanent part of that dumpster over there. Do you understand?"

The attacker could barely say yes.

"Is that your car over there in the NO PARKING zone?"

He nodded his head. Tiny called Ivan and told him what happened.

"I'll call the lieutenant and tell him. Good work, Tiny."

Ivan called the lieutenant right away and told him everything.

"Hold on for a minute Ivan, let me see how soon

Ramon and Ted can get there."

Ramon and Ted were at their desks and going over all the information they had on the robbery/assault case. The attacks were getting closer to their jurisdiction. The lieutenant waved them into his office and told them what had just happened.

"Take a break guys and take that scum off their hands."

"Ivan, Ramon and Ted should be there in about twenty minutes."

When Ramon and Ted arrived, they thanked Ivan and Tiny and told Mr. Robbins they were so glad he was okay. They both picked up the attacker under each arm and put him in their police car.

Ivan told them, "That's his car in the NO PARKING zone."

"We'll have it impounded, Ivan."

Ivan thanked them and they took off.

Mr. Robbins thanked Tiny again and again for helping him.

"If it hadn't been for you, Tiny I don't know what would have happened to me."

"No problem, Mr. Robbins. Now, go do your shopping and don't worry, I'll be close by. Any more problems, don't hesitate to call me or Ivan. I think we've seen the last of them."

CHAPTER 17

The next incident that occurred involved Carlos Mendoza, a drug leader who was in prison for the second time. The first time Carlos and his drug gang were incarcerated was when they had stored some of their drug merchandise in one of Donna's apartments. The authorities wanted to know if they had incarcerated the drug leader of the gang. Carlos told them no, but said a rival drug leader, Jose Rivera was actually their leader.

Carlos gave them Jose's office location. For his cooperation, Carlos was placed in the Witness Protection Program (WPP). The second time he was incarcerated was when he deserted the WPP and returned to California to continue to run his drug business and merge Jose's team into his own. He was caught by Eduardo Escobar, an undercover agent.

One morning as Carlos was entering the prison cafeteria he ran into Jose Rivera, the drug leader he had snitched on.

"Hi Jose, how are you doing?"

"I'm okay Carlos. I heard while I've been in here you took over my team."

"Yes, I did. I thought it was the least I could do for you."

"Well Carlos, that was very thoughtful of you."

Carlos gave Jose his biggest smile.

Jose said, "You know Carlos, if I am released before you, I will return the favor and do the same for you."

Jose saw the big smile on Carlos disappear instantly. They went through the food line together and sat down to eat their breakfast.

"Carlos, one question. Why did you go into the Witness Protection Program (WPP)?"

"As a means of escape from this place, Jose."

"I see."

"When I deserted the WPP Jose, I returned to California and heard they had incarcerated you. I thought I could be of help to you and encouraged your team to join mine."

"That was very considerate of you, Carlos."

"What are friends for, Jose?"

Jose was nobody's fool. It didn't take him long to figure out that Carlos had set him up. For his cooperation, Carlos was released into the WPP. Carlos was riding high when he was back in California until the hot shot undercover agent,

Eduardo Escobar infiltrated his team, and Carlos ended up incarcerated for a second time.

As the dining room was thinning out, Jose saw an old friend of his sitting at a table by himself, finishing his coffee. He went over and joined him. His friend, Gus had done quite a few contract hits for him.

"Hi Gus, how in the hell are you?"

"A lot better if I wasn't in here."

"What are you in for?"

"I was an innocent bystander during a small-time store robbery. A witness ID'd me. He couldn't see shit. He wore those thick coke bottle glasses. I don't think he could identify his own mother. How about you, Jose?"

"Similar situation. My attorney should have me out by Monday. Gus, I need you to do me a favor."

"What is it, Jose?"

"Did you see the guy sitting next to me at breakfast?"

"You mean Carlos?"

"Yes."

"A real asshole, Jose."

"I know."

"Can you take him out for me?"

"Sure, how soon?"

"ASAP. How much?"

"I'll need three G's."

"No problem. Do you still have the same account number?"

"I do."

"My CPA will deposit the money in your account twenty-four hours after it is done."

"He won't make dinner tomorrow night."

"Thank you, Gus."

Jose gave Gus his attorney's number.

"He'll help get you out of here. I'll tell him you'll call."

"Thanks, Jose."

"Anytime."

The next day, before dinner, the guards were monitoring the prisoners as they were coming in from the exercise yard. All of a sudden, there was a lot of noise and commotion. Carlos was down. He was face down on the ground in a large pool of blood. Someone had shanked him. Of course, no one had seen a thing, not even the guards.

CHAPTER 18

Jose had his drug headquarters in a high-rise office building. He leased two offices, each with a reserved parking space in the building. One office he used to run his drug business and was listed under a bogus name. The other office was used as a front for a legitimate business and was listed under his own name. All the files and computers in this office looked like he was running a legitimate business. The offices were located on different floors of the same building. Jose did this to throw off authorities in case of any interrogation. It had come in handy more than once and was well worth the extra cost. He had an answering service pick up any calls made to the legitimate office. Jose's secretary in his office under the bogus name monitored all calls made to the legitimate office. They would be answered accordingly.

Jose's attorney came to see him a few days before his hearing was due in court. Jose knew immediately by his attorney's smile that he would be walking out after the hearing. They spoke briefly. His attorney got up to leave, patted Jose on his back and whispered in his ear.

"No problem, as usual, Jose."

A few days later, Jose's hearing came up.

The bailiff called, "All rise. Court is in session."

Jose's case was the first one called. His attorney spoke first.

"Your honor, this case should have never happened. As you will see, the prosecution has absolutely no credible evidence, whatsoever. My client has been a law-abiding citizen in the community for the past year-and-a-half, actively involved in a legal business, as you can see by his office records and computer, which were confiscated by the authorities for the prosecution. How his name came up is a mystery. I ask for an immediate dismissal for my client based on insufficient evidence submitted by the prosecution."

The judge said, "After a thorough review of the prosecution's evidence, I completely agree with the defense. This case should have never come up."

He banged his gavel.

"This case is dismissed. You are free to go Mr. Rivera."

Jose and his attorney stood.

"Thank you, your honor."

The judge banged his gavel loudly, "Next!"

Jose thought, well I am three G's less, but at least Carlos won't be around to come up with any new schemes.

CHAPTER 19

There were no leads on the robbery and assault case for the next few weeks. Then one attempted robbery occurred in Long Beach with the same M.O. The woman screamed her head off when the intruder forced his way in. This was now in the lieutenant's jurisdiction. Ray flew the coop as fast as he could. It happened so fast she was unable to identify him.

Ramon and Ted were sitting at their desks studying all the information Ivan had given them and the map the lieutenant had given them at their morning meeting on the robbery assault case.

"Ted, what are we missing here? There's got to be a connection." They looked at the map again of the areas the lieutenant had pinpointed where the assailant had struck. The areas were very close to the Arizona/California border, then moved into Southern California. Then it hit Ramon. Ted, I think it's the location.

"Ted, let's look at the license plate Ivan gave us of that new guy in town. The car dealership on the plate is kind of blurry. Let's enlarge it and see if we can make it out?"

"The enlargement helped. I think we can almost make out the dealership name now. Let's see if we can find out where it's located."

It took a while, but they finally found the location. It was a small town in California very close to the Arizona border. Ramon's adrenaline rose.

"BINGO! Ted, let's call the owner there, and put him on the speaker phone."

Ted dialed the dealership. A voice answered, "Ben Harper here. Can I help you?"

Ramon identified himself.

"Mr. Harper, are you the owner?"

"Yes I am."

"Mr. Harper, we are currently working on a case and you may be able to help us with it."

"I'll certainly try."

"I'm going to fax you a picture of someone, Mr. Harper. Please tell me if you recognize him?"

Ramon faxed him the enlarged picture that Ivan had taken of Ray at Curly's. Mr. Harper came back on the line.

"Yes sir, he was here a few weeks ago and traded his car for one I had on my lot."

"What kind of car did he have, and what did he trade it in for?"

"He had a year-old Lexus in mint condition and traded it for a medium size, more economical car. I paid him cash for the difference."

"Do you still have the Lexus?"

"You bet. I am going to keep it for my own personal car. I have always wanted a Lexus."

"For our records, could you fax me the license plate and VIN number of both cars?"

"Yes, if you don't mind waiting on the line again."

"No problem."

He came back on the line.

"Did you receive the fax?"

"Yes, I did. Thank you, sir, for your cooperation. We will get back to you if we have any further questions."

Ramon said, "Ted, let's see what outstanding warrants they have in Arizona on a stolen Lexus. I have a good feeling about this. A recent warrant appeared on their screen involving an unsolved murder and a stolen Lexus."

Ted called the Arizona authorities and put them on the speaker phone. Ramon identified himself and asked to speak to the detective in charge of the open case involving a murder and a stolen Lexus. The detective told him about the case they were working on.

"The owner of a Lexus had recently advertised his car for sale at his home. A prospective buyer came by to see the car. He shot the owner point blank and stole his car. So far, we have no leads."

Ramon said, "We may be able to help. Do you have the license plate and VIN number of the Lexus?"

"We do. I'll fax it to you right now."

He faxed the numbers to Ramon.

"BINGO! Detective, we have a match for you!"

Ramon knocked on the lieutenant's door and he waved Ramon and Ted in.

"Lieutenant, we have something you won't believe. It looks like it might involve the suspect Ivan mentioned. Raymond Martin for the robbery-assault cases, and also an unsolved murder and stolen Lexus which occurred in Arizona."

"Tell me." Said the lieutenant.

Ramon explained everything to him.

"I'll put out a warrant to arrest Raymond Martin for murder right now, as well as, the stollen Lexus. Take a back-up with you."

The lieutenant gave the detectives the address of the motel where Ray was staying that Ivan had given him.

"Outstanding work guys."

The lieutenant called Ivan and told him the news.

"Ivan, I swear I'm going to have to put you on salary."

"Just helping out if I can lieutenant. I have a feeling that water glass with his DNA on it might help with the robbery-assault cases, too."

"You're incredible, Ivan."

"Ivan, Ramon and Ted are on their way to arrest him at his motel. He will be booked on murder and stolen car charges in Arizona and, also, held as a suspect in the robbery/assault cases here."

"Thank you again, Ivan."

"All in a day's work, lieutenant."

CHAPTER 20

When Ramon and Ted reached the motel, they identified themselves to the manager. The manager took them to Ray's room number and knocked on the door. Ramon and Ted drew their weapon's.

"Who is it?"

Ramon said, "The manager. We need to check out an electrical problem. It will only take a minute."

Ray opened the door slowly. Ramon pushed the door hard.

"Raymond Martin, you're under arrest. This is the police."

They cuffed him, read him his rights, and put him in their undercover car. Ray was silent all the way to the police station. After he was processed and put in a cell, the lieutenant said to Ramon and Ted, "Let's do a line up right away and see if any of the victims can ID him for the robbery assault cases. Maybe it will help jog someone's memory."

"We'll take care of it, lieutenant."

Ramon called the Arizona authorities in charge of the case and brought them up to date.

Ramon told them, "We have the suspect in custody now."

The lieutenant in charge in Arizona said, "We'll have a couple of our detectives out there late this afternoon. We'll interrogate him and take him off your hands and take him back to Arizona. Thank you for nailing this guy for us."

"You bet. We have a search warrant in process for his room in the motel where he is staying. Maybe we'll get lucky and find the murder weapon he used to shoot that poor guy."

"He is also a suspect here in a series of robbery/assault cases in Southern California. We will let you know as soon as we have more evidence in this area."

The detectives from Arizona, Frank and Jason, arrived at the LAPD station around 4:00p.m. Introductions were made and Raymond was brought to an interrogation room in cuffs and shackles.

Ramon and Ted had gotten their search warrant and were going over every niche of Raymond's motel room as he was being interrogated by the Arizona detectives. Ramon and Ted didn't find any evidence that would be helpful for their robbery/assault case, but they did find a bonus for Frank and Jason, the Arizona detectives. As Ramon was searching Raymond's duffel bag.

Ramon said, "Look what we have here! A gun, and it's the same make and model as the murder weapon." Ramon put the gun in an evidence bag for the Arizona detectives.

When Ramon and Ted returned to the station, Frank and Jason were finishing up their interrogation with Raymond.

Ramon said, "A present for you to take back to Arizona."

When Frank and Jason saw the gun in the evidence bag, they said, "We can't thank you guys enough. Thank you for your help again. This trip has been extremely worthwhile."

Frank and Jason took Raymond out in his cuffs and shackles. The lieutenant was glad their trip was successful and Raymond was gone. Before Raymond got in Frank and Jason's rental car to go to the airport, he said to Ramon, "You know I'm surprised you caught me. I have an IQ around 170. That's pretty close to a genius."

Ramon just looked at him in disgust.

"Is that a plus or a minus figure, Raymond?"

Before Frank and Jason got in the car, Ramon said, "Let us

know when you're ready for us to come out for his trial. Two of the victims he robbed and assaulted have just given a positive identification on him. We will probably find more evidence in the next few weeks. The DNA is still out. They always have a back-log, so that will take another week or so."

Ramon said, "Let's stay in touch. Have a good trip home."

"Thank you again."

Ramon had given them Ben Harper's dealership address and phone number. Their Arizona forensic team would probably want to see if there was any additional evidence on the Lexus, which might be helpful.

CHAPTER 21

The lieutenant called Ramon into his office. His partner, Ted was still on vacation.

"Ramon, I've assigned a new recruit for you."

"Oh? Will Ted and I still be partners?"

"Of course."

"Yes, I think you'll like your new recruit."

"What's he like?"

"Very big and strong, hairy, with large teeth, and big ears."

The lieutenant could see Ramon starting to squirm in his chair. The lieutenant couldn't contain himself any longer and he burst out laughing.

"Oh, Ramon, I forgot to tell you he has four legs. His name is Blitz and you will be his handler. He's a superstar in the K-9 unit just like you are here, Ramon. You're perfect for each other. Blitz is short for Blitzkrieg. That will give you some idea how fast and powerful he is."

"Lieutenant, I can hardly wait. You know how I love

dogs, especially big ones. How soon is this going to happen?"

"Right away. He's out on the training field waiting for you right now. He will be graduating in two weeks. Familiarize yourself with everything you need to know. As his handler, you will be taking him through his paces at graduation. Now go meet your buddy."

Ramon went over to the K-9's field. He saw his friend Eduardo Escobar, the undercover narcotics officer. Blitz was beside him. When he saw Blitz, Ramon was overwhelmed. He was huge, very handsome, with thick tan and black hair, and very intimidating looking. Eduardo was scratching Blitz's ears.

"Ramon, you are one lucky son-of-a-bitch."

"So I've heard."

Ramon started petting Blitz and talking to him, "Ok big guy, let's go."

He took Blitz's training book, put him on his lead and out they went out on to the field. They stayed in the background until the director motioned for Ramon to come over.

"Ramon, we will work with Blitz for about thirty minutes to give you an idea how he reacts. Then you can take him home. He's something else."

Ramon watched Blitz go through his paces and was amazed at how perfectly and quickly he responded to all the commands. When they were through, he called Sandy with all the news. He could hardly wait to get home with Blitz. When they arrived, Sandy met them at the door and greeted Blitz before Ramon.

Ramon laughed and said, "I guess I'm second fiddle now. Let's see what Angelina does."

Angelina was the little white Italian kitty Ted, his partner and wife, Janet had given them as a wedding present.

Sandy brought her out and introduced them right away. Ramon took Blitz's leash off and they sniffed noses and Blitz licked her face very gently.

"Oh, Ramon, I think they like each other. Angelina wants down."

Sandy put her down by Blitz and Angelina rubbed up against him.

"Sandy, what's that funny noise?"

"Oh, Ramon, she's purring."

"Sandy, let's go in by the fireplace and see if they follow us."

"Here they come, Ramon."

Blitz laid down by the warm fire and Angelina snuggled up against him.

"This is unbelievable, Ramon."

"I know, Sandy, I know."

"Honey, I thought of something they might really like. I'm going to go out and buy something for them, now. You stay here with them and I'll be back in about thirty minutes."

"What is it, Ramon?"

"I'll surprise all of you."

When he returned, Sandy saw Ramon struggling to get a very large bed in the house.

"Is that for you, Ramon?"

"Very funny, hold this door open for me."

Ramon carried the bed over by the fireplace. He spread out two large fluffy blankets in the bed, which he had also bought. Blitz got immediately in the bed and Angelina followed suit.

"I've got to get a picture of this, Sandy to show the lieutenant."

She laughed, "He won't believe this."

Blitz's graduation was coming up next weekend. Ramon and Sandy were more excited than Blitz was. The trainers and their dogs were on the training field and the bleachers were packed with friends and relatives. Each one went through their paces with all the commands and exercises. The program lasted about 3 hours. At the end a trophy was given to the most outstanding dog. Blitz came in first and won the top trophy hands down. He seemed to excel in every category. Ramon was so proud of him he couldn't see straight. When Sandy came running out to the field, she gave both of them a kiss, Blitz first, then Ramon. Then she gave Blitz a special treat.

Ramon said, "Where's my treat?"

Sandy smiled and said, "You'll get your treat later, Ramon."

"Promise?"

"You know I always keep my promises."

And she did.

CHAPTER 22

The lieutenant called Ramon at home to congratulate him.

"I heard Blitz won the top trophy."

"He sure did, lieutenant."

"How are Blitz and Angelina doing?"

"Well, they are inseparable. Sandy is convinced Angelina thinks Blitz is her mother."

The lieutenant started laughing.

"I'm anxious to see them, Ramon."

"You will, lieutenant, at our Christmas party."

CHAPTER 23

Sandy asked Ramon, "Are Ted and Janet back from vacation?"

"They just got back yesterday, but he's not due back in the office for a couple of days."

"Why don't we have them over tomorrow night for dinner."

"Good idea, Sandy."

"I can hardly wait for them to see Blitz and Angelina together, Ramon."

"Me too!"

"And we can hear all about their vacation."

"Does Chinese sound ok? That way we can spend more time with them. I'll have them deliver, ok."

"Sounds great Sandy, I'll call Ted now. How about tomorrow, 6:30 pm?"

"Perfect," she said.

"Hi Ted, it's Ramon. How was the trip?"

"Great."

"Sandy and I want to hear all about it. Can you and Janet come over for Chinese tomorrow night?"

"Yes."

"How about 6:30 pm?"

"That's perfect."

"How is my little Italian kitty, Angelina?" Ted was very proud of his Italian heritage.

"Just great, Ted. Have we got a surprise for you and Janet."

"We love surprises. See you tomorrow night."

Ramon was so proud of Blitz, he put his trophy on the mantle above the fireplace. He also framed his certificate from graduating first in his class in the K-9 unit and hung it on the wall close to the trophy.

Ted and Janet arrived exactly at 6:30 pm. They got the shock of their lives when Ramon opened the door. Standing next to Ramon was a huge German Shepard and Angelina was right beside him. Ted and Janet just stood there in shock.

"Come on in guys and I'll tell you the latest."

Ramon brought Ted up to date on everything he had missed out on at work.

Ted said, "It looks like Blitz and Angelina are inseparable."

Sandy said, "When Blitz is off duty, Angelina is always beside him. Angelina thinks Blitz is her mother."

They all laughed.

"Now tell us about your trip and then we will have our Chinese food." Ted and Janet loved the state of Idaho and went there frequently on vacation. They always stayed there with friends who lived in Ketchum, which was made famous by Ernest Hemingway.

"We went skiing almost every day in Sun Valley. The snow was perfect."

"Do you think you and Janet would like to live there when you retire?"

"We would love it. The question is could we afford it. We sure hope we will be able to."

CHAPTER 24

Rodger Henderson was a server at Breakers 9 restaurant, one of the best restaurants in San Pedro. The restaurant had a longtime reputation for its quality and fine dining. He has been working there almost five years. He was in his early thirties, nice looking guy with a friendly personality, but sometimes he could be a little too aggressive. He thought his future was looking bleaker by the day, working at the Breakers. His salary was nothing to brag about and the tips were okay sometimes and at other times not so hot. At the end on the month, he could barely make ends meet just for rent and a car payment. It was a lot of work with nothing to show for it. Hell, he didn't even have any insurance coverage. He was fed up with this kind of life.

A few years ago, Rodger used to crew on a large yacht. He had excellent boating skills and was also good at doing boating repairs. He had always loved the ocean and hoped one day he could afford to live on a power boat. Rodger was familiar with most of the marinas in San Pedro, but there was one small marina that caught his eye. It seemed very private and quiet. All of the power boats looked like they were about the same size, he guessed 35 feet or a little bit larger. He stopped one day to talk to the marina manager, Jim Porter.

"Jim, anything for sale that you know of?"

"Yes, a really nice power boat called Sandy's Getaway."

"Is it large enough to live on?"

"Yes. It's on gangway 15, slip 4."

"What's the size of most of the boats here, Jim?"

"About 40' and a little larger. We have a few live aboards. Actually, Sandy's Getaway is one of them. I can give you the number of the broker handling the sale."

"Thanks, that would be great."

Rodger had some savings put aside from his boat crewing days. It wouldn't hurt to check it out. Roger followed Jim's directions and went to Sandy's Getaway to check it out. It was exactly what he was looking for and it looked like it was in pretty good shape. He would give the broker a call.

He called the broker and made a low-ball offer on it. The offer was rejected. Rodger found out the hard way he couldn't qualify for a loan. His income was not enough, and he didn't have enough cash to put down. Rodger kept going back to the same marina. Maybe he could do some boat repairs to supplement his income. He saw right away that the name "Sandy's Getaway" had been changed to "Brian's Getaway". He saw a young man on-board doing some work, who might be the new owner. He walked down and introduced himself. They started talking and Brian invited him on board and offered him a beer. He told Rodger he was the new owner and was a full-time student at USC. An idea flashed through Rodger's mind.

"You know Brian, I am great at doing boat repairs from my days of yacht crewing."

He gave him his card he had from his boat crewing days.

"Anything you need or want to have done, maybe I can help."

"That's a great idea Rodger. Why don't you look around and make a list of anything that you think needs work?"

"In fact, Brian, I am free in the mornings and I can work part-time while you are at school. You can tell me what you would like me to do first."

"That's a great idea, Rodger."

"Do you have a spare locker where I can store my tools so I don't have to bring them every day?"

"Over there, Rodger." Brian pointed to a large locker.

"I never use that for anything. You are welcome to it. When you leave today, talk to Jim Porter, our marina manager. He will give you a form to fill out and he'll help get you certified." Brian said, "I'll call him now and tell him you'll be doing some work on my boat. That way you can be on the boat without me on board. And when Jim sees you, he'll know you're doing repairs and not an intruder."

Roger found that the extra income helped some by doing repairs on Brian's boat, but not enough. Rodger thought his future still looked pretty bleak.

CHAPTER 25

One night, one of Rodger's best customers at The Breakers asked him to join him for a drink after Rodger got off work. They met at an upscale bar and had a few drinks. His friend asked him if he might be interested in doing something else. It was a little risky, but paid extremely well. They discussed it and Rodger was excited about the opportunity, especially the financial upside. His friend said he would introduce him to someone higher up and he could go from there.

Rodger met the individual and liked everything he heard. He would start as a part time drug carrier or "mule" and eventually move up to full-time. As an extra bonus, he could purchase a certain amount of the drugs for his own personal use at a discounted price.

Rodger's part-time routes were a snap. Everything seemed to be going his way for a change. The money was incredible and they even gave him a good discount for his drugs of choice to be used for his personal use. They told him he was doing a great job and felt a full-time position would be available soon.

Three months later, Rodger's supplier called him in.

"We have a full-time position available for you now Rodger. Are you interested?"

"You bet!"

"Meet me for a drink tonight and I'll give you the details."

"Sounds good."

They met that night at the same upscale bar.

"Here is your new route, Rodger. Take a look at it. Do you have any questions?"

"Looks pretty straight forward."

"Good."

He told him what the financial increase would be as well as the bonus.

"What do you think?"

Rodger gulped and tried not to look surprised.

"I am very pleased. When would I start?"

"In a week."

"I will give notice tomorrow at The Breakers."

"Good. We look forward to having you on board."

They had a delicious dinner and his friend introduced him to a few other men there. When Rodger left, he felt like a different person, feeling on top of the world. As a full-time mule, Rodger's net worth started to increase rapidly. At the end of each delivery he would be paid with a large packet of high denomination bills. He could feel his dream of a nice sea craft becoming a reality. He might even be able to pay all cash for it.

Brian had given Rodger the only key he had for his locker to use to store his tools. When Rodger became a full-time "mule" or drug carrier, it was becoming impractical and not safe to have any drugs stored in his apartment, or a lot of cash. Then it occurred to him, why not use the locker Brian had given him to use on his boat? Rodger was the only one with access to the key. When Rodger's drug run schedule became a little tight, he got in the habit of returning to Brian's boat, which was closer than his apartment to spend the night. He would stash any drugs he had on him and large packets of cash in the locker. Whenever he had some spare time, he would take the cash and drop it off in his safety deposit box at the bank when they were open.

CHAPTER 26

There was only one way to describe the accommodations for his supplier's parties. They were massive and very secluded on large acres of land, located in a remote area a few miles outside of the city. Access was only permitted by going through an enormous iron gate monitored by heavily armed guards. Exquisite Spanish style haciendas stretched endlessly over the grounds appearing more like the grounds of a major hotel. They contained all types of facilities for their guests and every type of entertainment imaginable.

Roger was at an all-time high. He was now included in all of his supplier's extravagant parties since he was full-time. Busloads of gorgeous women would be dropped off for the men's entertainment. They were all knockouts, shapely, well-endowed and knew every trick in the book. He could choose anyone he wanted. Sometimes he would choose more than one at a time. Anything goes and he liked variety. There were tables and tables of exquisite food and all kinds of liquors and wines. Beluga caviar became a regular staple in his diet. Before he left, he would hit the dessert tables, which were unbelievable. He had never seen that many different desserts. Rodger loved life in the fast lane. And everything was paid for. La Dolce Vida!

His closet was now full of brand name clothes of all kinds, suits, shirts, sport clothes, shoes, etc. Most of his clothes were tailor made. He ordered expensive dress shirts to go with his new pants and expensive ties and handkerchiefs to go with the suits. His life had changed dramatically and he loved every minute of it.

Rodger was having a lot of experiences with a variety of women. However, he realized he hadn't been on an actual date in a long time. He remembered Andrea, a hostess at one of the five-star restaurants in town. She was very attractive and he had thought about asking her out before, but he didn't have much money then. He stopped in late one night and was having a drink at the bar. She walked by him.

"Hi Andrea, remember me, Rodger Henderson?"

"Sure, I do, Rodger."

He saw a Happy Birthday pin on her dress.

"Can I buy you a drink to celebrate your birthday, after you're off work? Maybe go to a jazz club and listen to a little music?"

"That sounds great. I'll come and get you at the bar Rodger, in about thirty minutes."

"Okay."

He spotted Andrea coming towards him shortly.

"I'm ready, Rodger."

The valet brought Rodger's brand-new black SUV around and they were off. The jazz club was only a few minutes away. When Rodger drove into the valet parking, Andrea said, "Oh, I love this place."

"Me too, Andrea."

The hostess took them to a cozy small table in a dark corner. The music started and was incredible. It was a small combo piano, bass, and drums with an outstanding female vocalist. Rodger ordered drinks for them and they selected various appetizers. They had another round of drinks and enjoyed the jazz until they were ready to close.

When they were leaving, Andrea said, "I can leave my car at work, Rodger."

They had such a nice evening at the jazz club, maybe she would ask him in for an after-dinner drink. He seemed very nice. She gave him her home address and when they arrived, she said, "Rodger, you can just park in my subterranean garage."

The garage was dark and so were Rodger's SUV windows. Andrea pointed to her parking spot and Rodger drove in.

"Let's get more comfortable, Andrea."

He pushed a button and her seat went down flat. He was on top of her in a second with his hands under her dress. He was pretty sure she was not wearing any underwear. She could feel his hardness pushing into her.

'Good grief,' she thought, 'this guy doesn't waste any time.' He reached for his zipper and started to slide it down.

"Uh, oh."

"What is it, Rodger?"

"My zipper is stuck. I can't force it. These pants are new and very expensive."

All of a sudden, she felt Rodger's "MR. HAPPY" go very limp. Andrea straightened out her dress, opened her side of the door, and stepped out of the SUV.

"Rodger, I'm going in."

She could hardly wait to get into her apartment.

"I've got an early day tomorrow, Rodger. I'm going to call it a night. Thank you again. Good night and good luck."

She felt like adding *and I hope I never see you again.*

She walked quickly to the elevator in her apartment building.

On his way home, Rodger was thinking, 'what an expensive night, and for what?' He could have his pick of any woman or more than one at a time at his supplier's parties. Plus, it didn't cost him a dime. Why bother to look any further. What a waste of time and money. He could have anything he wanted and more and it was free. When he got home, he could not get his zipper to budge. He had a terrible time getting out of his pants. It took him a good fifteen minutes! He would drop them off at the cleaners in the morning and they could fix his zipper.

Andrea was glad Rodger's zipper had gotten stuck. She felt this guy didn't really like women, he just liked to use them. Good riddance! Thank goodness she didn't give him her unlisted telephone number.

CHAPTER 27

It was Saturday morning.

Sandy said, "Ramon, I think I'll see if Brian is down at his boat. I haven't seen him for a while and I want to see how school is."

"Okay. I'm going to take Blitz for some exercise. We can try to meet you there."

As Sandy was coming down the gangway, she froze when she saw Rodger on Brian's boat. Brian introduced them.

"Sandy, this is Rodger. He's helping me do some repairs."

Roger was still helping Brian with any repairs he might need. But he was mainly using Brian's boat to store his drugs and cash.

"I've met Rodger before, Brian. In fact, he made an offer to buy my boat a while ago."

"Yes, he told me. Is Ramon with you, Sandy?"

"He'll be here shortly."

There was something about Rodger that Sandy didn't like

and she couldn't put her finger on it. Maybe his eyes. They seemed shifty. He never looked directly at you. Sandy had no idea that Brian knew Rodger, and Rodger had no idea that Brian and Sandy knew each other. Not only did they know each other, but they considered each other as family. Brian's family had actually rescued Sandy from foster homes. Rodger also did not know that Sandy's husband was an ace detective with the LAPD and was a handler for a superstar K-9 German Shepard.

It was time for Rodger to leave to make his drug delivery schedule.

Rodger said, "Got to run, Brian. See you in a couple of days. Bye Sandy."

Thirty minutes later, Brian saw Ramon and Blitz coming down the gangplank. Brian jumped off his boat and ran down the gangplank to greet them.

"Hi guys."

Brian loved Blitz and started petting and making a big fuss over him.

"Come aboard guys."

The minute Blitz was on board he immediately ran to the locker and went crazy. He started scratching and pawing at it frantically.

"What's the matter, Blitz?" Brian said, "Ramon, he's upset about something."

"Brian, from Blitz's reaction I'm afraid we are going to have to open that locker, under law. Do you have a key?"

"I gave my only key to Rodger."

"Do you have any bolt cutters on board?"

"I think so. Let me check down below. We're in luck, Ramon. I found some. Let me see if I can break that lock, Ramon."

Brian worked on it for about twenty minutes.

"Whew, I think I've almost got it."

The lock finally broke and Ramon helped Brian lift the heavy lid. Brian just stood there in shock when he saw the packages of drugs and large amounts of money stuffed in the locker.

"What the heck?"

"Looks like Rodger was using your locker, Brian, to store his drugs and cash. Maybe even selling some of this stuff."

"I can't believe he would do this. He told me he was keeping his tools in the locker."

Ramon said, "Good boy, Blitz."

Blitz was patiently waiting for his treat. Ramon handed him a large treat which Blitz proudly took and started munching on it.

"Brian, do you know where Rodger lives?"

"I'm sorry Ramon, but I don't."

"Can you call Jim Porter, your marina manager? Maybe he has his address."

Brian did so.

"I'm sorry Brian, I don't. He was going to give it to me and hasn't done so. Anything wrong?"

"Let me talk to Jim, Brian."

Ramon took the phone from him.

"This is Ramon, Jim. Can you come up here for a minute?"

"Sure, on my way."

When Jim got to the boat, Ramon explained everything to him.

"We will arrest Rodger as soon as possible. Jim, I'm going to have my office fax you a picture of Rodger for you to give to all of your shift managers. If he shows up, please call us immediately. What's your fax number?"

Jim gave it to him.

"Thank you, Jim. We will fax you his picture for your staff. I'm going to put all this stuff in a large evidence bag and remove it right now. Thank you, Jim, for your cooperation."

"Anytime, Ramon."

Ramon called his office. He told the lieutenant what had happened.

"Lieutenant, I need an address for this guy."

"Hold on Ramon, let us check his driver's license."

The lieutenant came back on the line shortly with an address, car make and model, license plate, and phone number.

"I will check out the address, lieutenant, on my way to drop off the evidence bags at the office. See you soon. Oh, can you fax an enlarged picture of Rodger from his driver's license to this fax number? Attention Jim Porter. He's the marina manager here. Thanks lieutenant."

"Brian, if you never use that locker for anything, you might want to get rid of it. That drug scent can be hard to get rid of."

"Good idea, Ramon."

"I think it will fit in my car with everything else. Can you help me carry it out to my car, while I'm here?"

"Thank you, Ramon. That would be great."

Ramon put on his gloves and removed everything in the locker to large evidence bags and put the bags in the trunk of his car.

"Sandy, I'll call you later."

"Honey, I think I'll stay here with Brian for a while before I go home."

Ramon said his good-byes and he and Blitz left. Sandy looked at Brian. He was still pretty shook up.

"Brian, what a day you've had! I think we could both use some beer and sandwiches. What do you think?"

"Boy, does that sound good, Sandy."

"I'll make the sandwiches; you open the beer."

"Deal."

Ramon drove to Rodger's address first. He saw Rodger's name and apartment number on the mailboxes. The manager was outside and he stopped to talk to him.

"Can I help you with something?"

"Maybe. I was just checking out the apartments here." Ramon noticed the apartment below Rodger's had a FOR RENT sign.

"I'm a writer and need to work in a quiet place."

"Well, you've come to the right place. The fellow that lives above this unit is hardly ever here. He leaves his place every day in the afternoon around two. Sometimes he returns home early in the morning, but lately he doesn't return until the next day around 1:45 in the afternoon. Probably has a new girlfriend. This rental will be available the first of the month if you would like to come back then, I can show it to you."

"I just might do that. Thank you, sir."

"You bet."

Ramon got in his car and took off for the office. He signed in and dropped off the evidence bags first, then went to see the lieutenant.

When Ramon got to his office, he saw his partner, Ted sitting in the lieutenant's office. The lieutenant waved Ramon in.

"I was just telling Ted all the details of what you've told me, Ramon. Sit down. How do you want to handle this, Ramon?"

"Okay lieutenant, This is all the information I've recently obtained. Rodger leaves his apartment around two in the afternoon to begin his drug pick-up and deliveries. I think we need three relay cars to follow him to as many of his destinations as possible. Ted and I will be in one of the cars with Blitz. We need to be at his apartment today at 1:30 before he leaves at 2:00. I think we should follow him to as many destinations as we can. If the areas become too remote and he could spot us too easily, we need to arrest him right away. How does that sound?"

The lieutenant and Ted both gave him the high sign.

"Just in case we lose him and he returns to his apartment or Brian's boat, we will need an undercover guy 24/7 at each location."

All of the detectives with their partners were in their three undercover cars at 1:30 pm sharp at Rodger's apartment. Rodger left his apartment right on schedule at 2:00 pm. Car #1 with Ramon, Ted and Blitz followed a few cars behind Rodger. Cars 2 and 3 pulled out a few minutes later. Ted kept cars 2 and 3 informed of their location at all times. When they reached the first destination, Ramon and Ted broke away, and #2 car followed Rodger to the next destination. This process continued with car #3 and they began again with car #1. They made a record of each supplier's location.

Ramon spoke to everyone.

"He's in an area now that's too easy for him to spot us. I'm going to pull him over now and arrest him. Let's box him in now."

Ramon put on his siren and lights and pulled Rodger over. He put the spotlight on him and his voice came over the loud speaker.

"Get out of the car with your hands-on top of your head."

Rodger was shaking so badly he could barely open his door and step out and then he did a very foolish thing. He took off running.

Rodger had won all kinds of track meets in college. He had seen Blitz in the car and know he would be after him, but maybe he would have a chance to outrun him.

Ramon and Ted were completely taken by surprise. Ramon gave a signal to Blitz and he took off after Rodger. It didn't take long for Blitz to catch up to Rodger. He literally flew through the air knocking Rodger face down on the ground. When Ramon and Ted finally caught up with them, Ramon had to restrain himself from breaking up laughing. Rodger was sprawled face down on the ground and Blitz was sitting on top of Rodger's back proudly waiting for Ramon and his treat.

"Ted, look at this."

"Unbelievable."

"Could you take a picture for me?"

"Ramon, I wouldn't miss this one for anything."

"Thanks Ted. God, I love this dog."

"Ted, I can hardly wait to enlarge this picture, and frame it."

Ramon called Blitz off Rodger.

"Good boy, Blitz."

Ramon gave Blitz an extra-large treat. Rodger stood up shakily.

Ramon said, "Guard Blitz."

Blitz sat directly in front of Rodger, making low guttural sounds. Trembling, Rodger said to Ramon.

"He won't bite me, will he? He keeps curling up his lips. God, his teeth are huge."

"He just wants you to see what big teeth he has! You are under arrest, Rodger. Place your hands behind your back."

Ramon handcuffed him and read him his rights.

The other detectives got out of their cars and began searching Rodger's SUV. They found what they were looking for. Plenty of evidence, large amounts of drugs and cash from each location he had been to.

Ramon called the lieutenant and told him the good news.

"I think we have most of the locations of Rodger's pick-ups and deliveries. Now we have to interrogate him to see what we are up against at each of the locations. We are bringing him in now."

"Good work, guys."

Rodger was led into the interrogation room. The lieutenant was behind the invisible glass mirror, listening. Ramon sat across from Rodger.

"Rodger, how and where did you meet your connection before you became a mule?"

"Detective, I would like to call my lawyer first before

I answer any of your questions."

"Rodger that is your right. However, I would like to make one thing perfectly clear. If you cooperate with us, we can probably lessen your sentence. Otherwise, I can assure you, you will undoubtedly do time because of the evidence we have. Also, as you know, people in prisons are not the friendliest and drug suppliers do not like to leave any loose ends. Am I making myself perfectly clear?"

"Yes sir. Before I call my lawyer, could you tell me what information you want from me?"

"Yes, to some degree. The first question I asked you. Who was your connection, initially? How many supplier locations do they have? What are the supplier's names and also, how many mules do they have that you know about? How many workers at each location and how are they armed? Is there a central meeting place for all of you where you can get together informally and party and where is it located? These are some of the things we need to know. If you cooperate with us, we can help each other. This would also be considerably safer for you. As I mentioned before, these people do not like loose ends."

"Could you give me a little time to think about this?"

"Only until 7:00 am tomorrow morning. That will give you tonight to think about this. We can put you in a cell by yourself in the county jail so nobody will know you are here. This will be much safer for you. I hope you make the right decision, Rodger."

Ramon waved to the jailer waiting outside the locked door

and he led Rodger away. Ramon and Ted got together with the lieutenant in his office afterward.

"Lieutenant, I think we need to think about all this before we see Rodger at 7:00 in the morning."

"What are you thinking, Ramon?"

"Rodger seemed to make all his deliveries but the last one. His supplier is going to wonder what happened. Since he hasn't heard from Rodger, he will probably assume he got sick, was in a car accident, his car was stolen and so on. This will buy us some time with getting answers from Rodger and also giving SWAT time to set up their people to take down the locations."

"I like it, Ramon. Let's do it."

"Let's hope we get a positive response from Rodger at 7:00 am tomorrow morning."

Rodger's connection called the main supplier.

"Rodger didn't make his last delivery today."

"Do we know what happened?"

"Not yet. It could be any number of things. He could have gotten sick, had his car stolen, or maybe even gotten a ticket. I doubt the latter, he's got a great driving record."

"Let's give it 24 hours, then let's start calling some of the hospitals in the areas where he made his last delivery."

"Okay."

"Get back to me if you hear anything."

"Will do."

"Have someone stake out his apartment in the meantime."

"Okay, will do."

CHAPTER 28

One of the drug supplier's aides was ordered to check out the nearest hospital parking lot closest to Rodger's last delivery to see if he could spot Rodger's SUV. He was unsuccessful. However, the supplier was glad Rodger was very careful and had everything concealed in his trunk under lock and key in large suitcases. There was a built-in compartment in the bottom of each suitcase where the drugs and cash were stored. Clothes covered the compartments top in case he was ever searched. It looked like he was taking a trip. Rodger always felt the police might stop him for something.

At 7:00 am the next morning, the lieutenant and Ramon met with Rodger.

"What have you decided, Rodger?"

"If I tell you everything I know, what will happen to me?"

"You will be placed in our Witness Protection Program, (WPP) and your physical features will be slightly altered so no one will recognize you. You will be sent to another state to live. You will never have any connections with any of your friends or relatives you might have."

"When will this happen?"

"Immediately."

"I want to do it, detective."

"Good. We understand you like to be close to the water. Florida might be a good place to start your life over."

"I think Florida would be a good place for me. I will tell you everything I know."

"You made a very wise decision, Rodger."

For the next few hours Rodger told them everything they had asked for.

"Okay guys, we have a go ahead for the WPP Program for Rodger. Get a bulletin out immediately in the newspapers and also T.V. Run it daily for about a week. Show a picture of Rodger from his driver's license and say that he was fatally shot and left by the side of the highway by an unknown assailant. Give the highway and location, state, and approximate time. Also, give the model and type of his SUV, license plate, color, etc. He may have stopped to change a flat or gotten out of his car for some other reason. The assailant stole his SUV. Give our police hot line number here to call for anyone having any additional information."

Rodger's main supplier was avidly watching the T.V. bulletin about the shooting death of Rodger. He didn't get a chance to hear the newscaster finish his story. All hell broke loose at each of the supplier's locations when they were hit simultaneously by SWAT teams and everyone was arrested.

The lieutenant called Ramon and Ted into his office.

"You guys have done one hell of a job. The SWAT teams were successful. They hit each location you gave them simultaneously. Outstanding work, guys."

"Thank you, lieutenant."

"Surprised the hell out of them. There were a few casualties on our side, but nothing serious. They lost a total of ten men. The rest have been incarcerated."

"How long will it take to remove all the evidence from each location, lieutenant?"

"Probably a couple of days with several shifts working around the clock. Okay guys, I think our work for now is done. I think we need to celebrate. Let's go have a few pitchers of beer and something to eat."

Ramon and Ted chimed in, "Great idea, lieutenant," and off they went.

CHAPTER 29

Ivan decided to befriend Leo, a tenant in one of Donna's apartments. He used to be one of their worst trouble makers. But Ivan saw something in him that the others didn't see. Maybe Leo reminded him of himself a long, long time ago. Little by little, Ivan started to win Leo over and they became friends. One day, Ivan asked Leo a question.

"Leo, I have some difficult work to do today. Would you be willing to help me? I'll make it worth your while."

"Why me, Ivan?"

"Well I need someone in good physical shape and you look like you're not afraid of a little hard work."

"What's in it for me?"

"I can pay you fifteen dollars an hour."

"Okay, Ivan."

When they finished the work, Ivan said, "Great job, Leo. Thanks for helping me."

A few days later, Leo asked Ivan, "If there is anything else I can help you with Ivan, let me know."

"I sure will, Leo. I have some other things coming up soon. I like your work."

"Thank you, Ivan."

"Leo, I have a couple of meal tickets to Curly's Bar and Grill for you."

"I love Curly's. Thanks Ivan. I usually can't afford to eat there."

"Well Leo, now you can."

Curly's had the best comfort food in town, hands down. Ivan began to see Leo there more and more frequently. Sometimes with a lady friend. Instead of hitting the bars like he used to and causing trouble at Donna's apartments, Leo seemed to have a more positive attitude. He even started taking better care of himself.

One day when Ivan and Leo were chatting, Ivan asked him, "Leo, do you like to ride bikes?"

"You bet I do. I used to have a Harley, but then I ran into some hard times and had to sell it."

"Is your biker license still up to date?"

"Yes, it is."

"Do you have a helmet?"

"Yes, I kept my old one."

"Good."

"Are you familiar with our biker group, Leo?"

"Not really."

"Well, we are having a meeting in a few days. I would like for you to come."

Leo said, "Is it close by?"

"Not that far. I have a spare Harley you can use to get there."

Leo couldn't believe it. He smiled from ear to ear. Ivan gave him the meeting location and also his spare bike. Leo couldn't get over how much Ivan trusted him. He came to the meeting and Ivan introduced him to the other members. They made him feel welcome and he started to become interested in the group.

The next day, Ivan ran into Leo at Curly's.

"Hi Leo, what did you think of our meeting?"

"I really enjoyed the guys and talking to them."

"They would like you to come to our next meeting, Leo."

"Really?"

"They really liked you. Why don't you keep the bike for a while, Leo?"

"Are you sure?"

"Absolutely. Enjoy it Leo. It needs to be driven. Here is a spare key for the storage room. You can keep the bike in there for security."

"I'll keep good care of it, Ivan."

"I know you will, Leo."

"Leo, we're having a beach party this Saturday. We would like for you to come. Please feel free to bring a date."

"What can we bring, Ivan?"

"Not a thing. Just yourself. There's enough hot dogs and beer for everyone."

"Oh Leo, be sure you have an email address set up right away if you don't have one. It's the easiest way to keep in touch with the guys in our group. They will let you know what jobs are available and who could use some help. Here is a list for you of their names and emails. Let them know your email address right away so you can get involved in more work with them."

Leo respected the biker group and liked the work they did for those in need in the community. His life was changing rapidly for the better. He had a positive attitude and seemed to thrive on the work he did with Ivan's biker group. His life now seemed to have a purpose with new meaning. But most of all, Leo felt needed.

Ivan took Leo aside, "Leo, you're doing great work. I think you're going to be surprised at how much money you're going to make with your capabilities.

"How did you learn how to do all this?"

"Growing up, my father used to build houses and taught me a lot."

"You're pretty impressive, Leo. When you're ready, I would like to introduce you to my bank manager. He can set up some accounts for you Leo, at no charge which will be very beneficial for you. What do you think?"

"What kind of accounts, Ivan?"

"How about checking and savings?"

"I would like that Ivan, Thank you."

When Ivan went to work for Donna, he remembered she had helped him set up some accounts at her bank. He would do the same for Leo.

"Ivan, could I ask you a personal question?"

"Sure, Leo."

"Well, you know life is funny sometimes. You seem to have it all together. I was just wondering if there was a person or something that you attribute this to?"

"Yes Leo, I can. Without a doubt, Donna and her husband, Lieutenant Stephen McClary, have been very instrumental in so many ways. I know you and Donna got off to a bad start and I'm sorry about that, but I believe in that old saying, 'Sometimes you just have to let bygones be bygones.' What's past is in the past. Sometimes things are never as bad as they seem."

"You have a point, Ivan. Thank you for telling me this."

"Anytime, Leo."

CHAPTER 30

As Donna was running some errands in town one morning, she saw a couple of bikers ahead of her. One she knew was Ivan, the other she didn't recognize. Probably one of his biker buddies. She pulled into the post office and she saw them park their bikes across the street in front of Curly's. Must be going to breakfast, she thought. When the biker she didn't recognize took off his helmet she did a double take. It looked like Leo. Kind of, only this guy was well groomed and rather nice-looking. Curiosity got the best of her and she called Ivan later.

"Ivan, this is Donna. I could have sworn I saw you and Leo go into Curly's this morning. Were my eyes playing tricks on me?"

"No, they were not, Donna. That was really Leo."

"What happened?"

"Well, he's changed a lot and has been helping me do some work on your apartments."

"Like what?"

"Well, that drug gang that was in 2B made a mess of the place. A lot of work needed to be done. You wouldn't recognize it now. I can actually advertise it for rent now. Leo helped me with most of it."

"I can't believe it Ivan. That's wonderful. I can hardly wait to tell Stephen when he comes home."

Stephen, the lieutenant at the LAPD, told Leo a few months ago if he did one more thing to cause trouble at Donna's apartments, he would put him in jail immediately. Leo had always been a big troublemaker at Donna's apartments. At one time Leo even considered getting rid of Donna permanently. He and Donna never did see eye to eye.

"Stephen will be very pleased to hear this, Ivan. I guess people can change! Otherwise there would not be psychologists and psychiatrists."

"In this case Donna, Leo has definitely changed and definitely for the better. He's even becoming a regular at our biker meetings."

Donna said, "This is unbelievable. Stephen will be shocked."

When Stephen came home and they were eating dinner, Donna said, "Okay Stephen, brace yourself. I have something to tell you about Leo. You're never going to believe this."

"He's not causing you trouble again, is he?"

"No, no. Nothing like that."

Donna told him about everything she had seen that morning. She saw the look of shock on Stephen's face.

"This is incredible, Donna."

"I could hardly wait to tell you. I talked to Ivan. Leo's changed, Stephen. He's been helping Ivan and his biker buddies with their work. They have just recruited him into their group."

"I'm speechless, Donna."

"And you know who we have to thank for that, Stephen."

"Ivan. As we've said many times before Stephen, what would we do without him."

"I really don't know."

CHAPTER 31

Jeffery Ellis was in his old neighborhood one morning. He caught a glimpse of Ivan leaving Donna's apartments. Someone was with him on another Harley. He thought the guy almost looked like Leo, except this guy was clean cut. He did a double take. It was Leo! What the hell was going on? Ivan had gotten rid of all the tenants that he had considered riff raff and undesirables in Donna's apartments, which included Jeffery. Now all of a sudden Leo, who was the most troublesome of all the tenants was buddy-buddy with Ivan. What the hell was that all about? Jeffery was fuming. He wondered where Leo got the money for the bike and where did he keep it? He thought about it. Maybe in the store room of Donna's apartment. He would have to check that out. He was pretty good at picking locks. If the bike was there, he had an idea what he could do with it just for spite.

Jeffery needed to talk to someone who was savvier about Harley's than he was. A friend of his, Eddie had a Harley. Jeffery called him.

"I have a few questions about Harley's and I know you can help me. I'll spring for a couple of pitchers of beer."

"Sure Jeffery. At our favorite watering hole?"

"No, I moved and I go to Jake's now."

"I know Jake's. I can leave now and be there in about twenty minutes."

"Great, see you there, Eddie."

Jeffery saw Eddie's Harley in the parking lot when he got to Jake's. When he walked in, he saw Eddie seated in a back booth facing the door. Jeffery signaled the waitress for a pitcher of beer. She placed two frosty mugs and a large pitcher of beer with some nuts on the table.

They talked for a while and enjoyed their beers.

"Okay Jeffery, what questions do you have for me?"

Jeffery told him.

"No problem. When we're ready to leave, we'll go out to the parking lot and I'll show you how to jimmy the locks first, then get the bike going. You used to have a bike, right?"

"I did, but not a Harley."

"I don't think you'll have any problem. Piece of cake."

When they were in the parking lot, Eddie went over how to jimmy the locks.

"Here are the keys, Jeffery, drive it a short distance just to see if you have any more questions."

When he returned, Jeffery said, "Nice bike, Eddie."

"Do I know who's bike you are going to steal, Jeffery?"

"No, I don't think so. Better that you don't know."

Jeffery felt very confident about stealing the bike, however, he made one very critical mistake. He didn't realize the bike Leo was riding was owned by Ivan and not Leo. Nobody, but nobody messes with Ivan's Harleys and gets away with it.

CHAPTER 32

The next morning Leo had an early appointment and went down to the store room to get the Harley Ivan had loaned him. He froze in his tracks when he saw the lock on the door. Someone had picked it. A cold chill ran over him as he opened the door. Ivan's bike was gone! Panicking, he called Ivan immediately.

"Ivan, someone stole the bike."

"Stay there Leo, I'll be right over."

"Leo, can you think of anyone that might have ill feelings towards you or perhaps might be jealous?"

"Not off hand, Ivan."

"If anyone comes to mind, let me know right away."

"I will, Ivan."

Ivan thought about it over lunch and called his friend, the lieutenant.

"Lieutenant, this is Ivan."

"Hi Ivan, what's up?"

"Remember that tenant in one of Donna's apartments that robbed the liquor store? To lessen his sentence, didn't he tell you that Leo Garcia told him that he had been offered money to off Donna one time?"

"I do. It was Jeff Ellis."

"Could you do me a favor and fax me a photo of Jeff Ellis from his driver's license since he has a record with you?"

"Of course, Ivan. What's up?"

"I think he may have stolen one of my Harley's and I'm not sure where he lives now since he is no longer a tenant in Donna's apartments."

"You'll have his photo in a few minutes, Ivan. Can we help in any way?"

"I'll let you know, lieutenant."

CHAPTER 33

"Leo, do you think Jeffery Ellis still goes to the same bar the two of you used to go to?"

"I don't think so, but let me ask around. Do you think he might have something to do with this, Ivan?"

"Maybe, I'll let you know, Leo."

The next day, Leo told Ivan Jeffery was going to a bar called Jake's. He was usually there between one and three in the afternoon.

"Thank you, Leo."

Ivan called one of his bikers, Tiny.

"Tiny, I need you to find where this person lives now. He gave him the enlarged photo of Jeffery he had received from the lieutenant. I've heard he frequents a bar called Jake's."

"I know it, Ivan."

"Good. He usually goes there between 1 and 3 in the afternoon. When you see him, follow him to his new address. Use our company car so he won't spot you. Call me right away when you find out where he is living."

"Okay, Ivan."

Tiny called him the next day after 3:00 in the afternoon.

"Ivan, it looks like he is renting a room in a house."

He gave Ivan the address.

"Are you there now, Tiny?"

"Yes, I am. I am looking for your other motorcycle, right?"

"Yep."

"Wait a minute, the garage door is open and I can see a motorcycle there partially covered up."

"Can you read the license plate?"

He gave him what he could read.

"Great job, Tiny. Thank you, that's exactly what I needed."

Ivan called the lieutenant.

"Lieutenant, I believe Jeff Ellis stole my other Harley. It's in the garage of the house where he is currently renting a room. I can take it back illegally or would you prefer to take care of it legally?"

"We will take care of it right away for you, Ivan.

You're one of my best detectives and I don't want you getting arrested for breaking and entering. I'll call you when we have your bike."

Ivan gave him the license plate number of his bike and the house address where Jeff was staying. The lieutenant called him later that day.

"Will you be at Donna's apartments in about an hour, Ivan?"

"Yes."

"We have your bike and can drop it off to you in about an hour."

"Thank you, lieutenant."

Ivan called Leo and told him the good news.

"Let's go by one of the security stores in town and got an extra good lock and camera for surveillance. You can help me install this in the storage room, Leo."

The police dropped off his bike an hour later.

CHAPTER 34

Later, Ivan asked the lieutenant what happened to Jeffery.

"We charged him accordingly and put him in a cell with one of our friendlier cellmates if you know what I mean. Once he's out, I don't think he will be too anxious to return."

"Thank you, lieutenant."

CHAPTER 35

Even though Sandy Grant now lived in Southern California, her closest friends were still Alecia Bowers and her son, Brian in Northern California. Alecia and Sandy were like sisters. Alecia was also a widow whose husband had died of an infection a few years ago. Her son, Brian was now enrolled as a junior at USC on a scholarship program.

After Sandy's husband's death, she was alone and very vulnerable. That was when she met David Collins, who was still married to Donna, and had a serious affair with him, or so she thought. After David abruptly ended the affair, Sandy fell off a steep cliff on the Collin's property in Palos Verdes. She was mistakenly pronounced dead. It was questionable if she fell or was pushed.

After months and months of painful surgeries she recovered. She and Donna were no longer look-alikes, but Sandy was just as beautiful as ever. Her life began to change for the better when she met Ramon, Lieutenant McClary's ace detective, and they fell in love. She and Ramon married and they lived in his house in a nice part of San Pedro.

Sandy texted Alecia,

"Alecia, Ramon and I can hardly wait for you and your parents to come and celebrate the holidays with us. Let me know when you'll be arriving at LAX. We'll pick you up. We have plenty of room at our house and insist you all stay with us. Ramon can hardly wait to meet your parents.

All our love,

Sandy and Ramon"

Alecia texted back,

"Sandy, are you sure this won't be an imposition for all of us to stay with you and Ramon?

Love,

Alecia, Mom and Dad"

Sandy texted back,

"Are you kidding? Our feelings will be hurt if all of you don't stay with us. We have room for Brian too, but I think he wants to stay on his boat.

Love,

Sandy and Ramon"

Later, Alecia texted Sandy,

"Sandy, I have some extra vacation time accrued and can come a couple of weeks early, before my parents. Would that be okay? I can stay on Brian's boat."

Sandy texted back,

"No way! You are staying with me and Ramon in our home. Period. No ifs ands or buts. Alecia, this is great news. I am off work also so we can have a ball. I can hardly wait for you to get here."

"Okay, Sandy. My parents are still planning to arrive the week before Christmas."

"Good, Alecia, Ramon and I can hardly wait to see them. Text me when you have a date and arrival time and Ramon and I will pick you up at LAX."

CHAPTER 36

When Alecia arrived, she and Sandy got caught up on everything. Especially Alecia's love life. After she arrived, Sandy asked her if anything was new in the romance department.

"What happened with Brian's Health and Fitness professor?"

"Not much. A big fat zero."

Brian, Alecia's son had introduced her to one of his favorite professors at USC.

"Did you like him, Alecia?"

"He's nice, but no dice."

"Okay, I'm missing something here. You don't sound very excited."

"I met him for a cup of coffee last time I was here. Believe me, once was enough! He started telling me what vegetables I should eat and which ones I should avoid. Then he even made out a list for me. He said next time he would tell me about how to stay fit. I thought I was going to have to call 911 to resuscitate me. Everything was getting blurry."

"Well Alecia, just to warn you in advance, Brian wanted me to invite him to our Christmas party. I wonder if he'll bring a date?"

"He'll probably bring a vegetable, Sandy."

Sandy burst out laughing.

"Alecia, you know someone as pretty and nice as you is not going to be alone for too long."

"I hope you're right, Sandy."

CHAPTER 37

The next day, Sandy and Alecia decided to surprise Brian and decorate his boat for the holidays while he was studying. They bought him his favorite lunch, a Double-Double cheeseburger, large fries and a chocolate malt. What could be better? While Alecia was picking up his lunch, Sandy went next door to the deli to pick up some wine and all kinds of appetizers for Brian to have on his boat for the holidays. Brian's refrigerator was always empty. She put everything in her roll-away cart and off they went. As they passed the marina office, Jim Porter, the marina manager, waved at Sandy and motioned her over.

Alecia said, "Now that's someone I find very attractive, Sandy. I wonder if he is available?"

"I'll see what I can find out, Alecia. Why don't you take Brian's lunch down to him, and I'll be along in a few minutes with the rest of the stuff after I see what Jim wants."

"Okay."

"Hi Jim, what's up?"

"Hi Sandy, I just wanted to ask you something."

"Okay."

"I've been a widower for the past five years and find Brian's mom, Alecia and your close friend very attractive. Do you think she would consider going out with me for a nice dinner while she is here?"

Sandy's mind was racing.

"Tell you what, Jim. Alecia and I are decorating Brian's boat for the holidays. We should be done in about an hour. Why don't you join us for an early celebration on the boat? We've got some good appetizers and wine. How does that sound?"

"I would love that, Sandy. What can I bring?"

"Just yourself, Jim. This will give you an opportunity to ask Alecia yourself if she would like to go to dinner."

Sandy could hardly wait to tell Alecia when she reached the boat.

CHAPTER 38

"Guess what, Alecia?"

"What?"

"Jim wanted to ask me about you."

"Really?"

"Yes, he's been a widower for the past five years and finds you very attractive. He wants to know if you might consider letting him take you to dinner. I invited him down to the boat for a little holiday celebration of wine and appetizers. He will be here in about an hour, so let's get busy and get this boat decorated."

"That's great, Sandy."

Brian was just about done with his studying, when Alecia hollered down to him.

"Brian, come up here, we have something to show you."

Sandy flipped on the bright lights.

"Wow, this is incredible! I've got the best-looking boat in the marina."

Brian noticed the deck table laid out with all kinds of appetizers and wine.

"Brian, Jim Porter is coming down to help us celebrate. He should be here any minute. Here he comes now. I don't think he has met your mother."

"Hi everyone. Your boat looks fantastic, Brian."

He handed Brian a couple of bottles of very good wine, a red and a white.

"Jim, I don't think you have formally met my mother, Alecia."

"No, I haven't and the pleasure is all mine."

"I understand your parents will also be here in a couple of weeks, Alecia?"

"Yes, they will be, Jim."

"How long do you intend to stay?"

"We will go back about a week after New Year's."

"I see."

They all toasted to the holidays. They enjoyed each other's company and had a great time.

Sandy thought Jim was very likeable and a rugged, good-looking guy. He was in his early fifties, very tan and in good physical shape from being outside all day. She could see why Alecia found him so attractive. Sandy thought this might really work out for the two of them. She could hardly wait to tell Ramon.

Jim said, "Alecia, it is so nice to meet you. I have seen you a few times when you have visited Brian and Sandy. I would really like to get to know you better. Would you consider having dinner with me while you are here?"

"Why yes I would, Jim."

"Do you like Italian food?"

"I love it."

"I have a favorite Italian restaurant in San Pedro, Giovanni's. The food and wines are superb. Since you're staying such a short time, would you like to go there tomorrow night with me?"

"Yes, I would. Sounds great."

"How about 6:30 pm?"

"Perfect."

"Jim, since Alecia is staying with Ramon and me, why don't you come a little early to our house and we can all have a drink together before the two of you go to dinner?"

"That sounds great, Sandy."

"How does 6:00 pm sound?"

"That's perfect, Sandy."

She gave Jim their address.

"See you tomorrow night, Jim."

CHAPTER 39

As Jim and Alecia arrived at the restaurant, a valet met them and took Jim's car. Alecia was impressed when she saw how beautifully the outside of the restaurant was decorated with soft colored lights. She could also hear beautiful authentic Italian music coming from inside. Giovanni, the owner greeted them at the door and Jim introduced Alecia to him. Everyone spoke Italian, except Alecia. Giovanni brought them a bottle of special Italian Prosecco with a tray of delicious assorted appetizers to start with. Later, Jim selected what they would have for dinner with Giovanni's recommendations. Everything was superb.

After dinner, Alecia noted the music became more romantic and she and Jim took advantage of the dance floor they had. They both loved to dance and did so until the restaurant closed. When Jim took Alecia back to Sandy and Ramon's, he did not want to appear to be too forward and gave her a polite kiss on the cheek, thanking her for a wonderful evening.

CHAPTER 40

The next day, a small bouquet of beautiful roses arrived for her with a personal note, telling her how much he enjoyed their evening together. Alecia was knocked out.

Sandy and Ramon invited Jim over for dinner the following evening. Jim had spent the day planning activities with Alecia for the rest of the week. They were becoming inseparable.

Once in a blue moon you meet someone and something just clicks. It doesn't happen very often, but when it does, you never forget it. That is exactly what happened to Jim and Alecia.

"Ramon, I'm so happy for them. They are crazy about one another."

The next night Jim asked Alecia if she would like to have Chinese food at his home.

"I would love that, Jim."

Jim's home was in a beautiful neighborhood of San Pedro. His home was very attractive and surprisingly large. He built a nice fire in the den and made them before dinner drinks. The Chinese food was delivered and delicious. Afterwards, he sat on the couch next to her and they had an after dinner Chinese liquor.

"I think you'll like this."

"It's very tasty. What is in it?"

"I have no idea, but it's a very good liquor with a little of this and a little of that."

He put on some soft music and they moved closer to one another.

"I'm so glad we finally met, Alecia."

"Me too, Jim."

He kissed her lightly on the mouth then they became more intimate and their kisses more passionate. He held her very close. His hand began to fondle her breasts. Then he put his hand between her legs and put her hand on his hardness. She started to moan with desire, her body against his.

"I want you, Alecia. Come."

He stood up, took her by her hand and led her into his bedroom.

She thought, 'What the hell? It's been a long time.'

Slowly he started unbuttoning her blouse and then removed her bra.

"You're beautiful, Alecia."

Then he unzipped her pants and removed them. He brought her hands up to his shirt and she removed his shirt. Then she helped him unzip his pants.

"Jim, I have to warn you, I'm a little out of practice."

"Believe me Alecia, this is one thing you never forget."

He laid her down on his bed and started caressing her. She could feel his hardness against her body. She opened her legs wide and he moved his head downward. Alecia began to tremble with desire. He started doing incredible things to her and she started to lose control.

Alecia gasped, "Now, Jim, now."

He moved upward, and she could feel him begin to enter her, slowly at first, then deeper and deeper. They began moving together faster and faster. She was losing all control and started having one orgasm after another. Then they both climaxed. They couldn't seem to get enough of each other. This went on and on until they were both so exhausted, they had to rest.

"Alecia, you are incredible. I didn't mean for this to happen so soon, but I couldn't stop myself. I wanted you so much."

"I felt the same way, Jim."

"I really don't want to take you back to Sandy and Ramon's tonight. I'd like to take you to Catalina tomorrow and we can stay all night there. How does that sound?"

"You talked me into it."

"We can pretend we missed the last boat. Do you think they would believe that?"

"Not really, but it sounds good."

"I'll call early tomorrow and make a hotel reservation for a couple of days and then we can go over on the Catalina Express Boat that leaves from San Pedro. I'll pick you up about 9:00 am."

"Sounds good. All casual things, right?"

"Uh-huh."

CHAPTER 41

The next morning Sandy said, "Alecia, what do you have planned for the day?"

"Jim and I are going to Catalina."

"Ramon and I love it over there, Alecia. We would have gone with you."

"That's alright, maybe next time."

"Oh, I get it. You two want to be alone."

"Uh-huh."

"Well, you will love it over there. As long as you're going, it's too bad you're not staying over."

"Promise not to tell anyone, Sandy, but that's exactly what we intend to do. When we're not back, could you tell everyone that we missed the last boat?"

"Got it, Alecia."

Sandy could hardly wait for Ramon to come home to tell him the latest.

CHAPTER 42

Eva, Brian's ex-girlfriend, went to her father's study after dinner one night.

"Hi Daddy, do you have a few minutes for me?"

"I always have time for my Eva. What's up?"

"Well, you know I'll be graduating next year and I wanted to ask you if I could have my graduation present a little early?"

"What do you have in mind?"

"You know I excelled in all the boating classes at the marina and I love being on the water."

"Are you still seeing your friend Brian?"

"Off and on, but nothing serious."

Her father had no idea Brian had ended the relationship.

"I saw a great little power boat for sale the other day. I would love to have it, but I wanted to see what you thought. She knew the price would hardly make a dent in his finances. The owner is being transferred in his job and has to sell it. I made a list of the important specifics for you."

"Good, let me see what you have."

She showed him some large photos.

"Very nice, hon."

"He's asking for $70,000. I've researched the price and it's comparable to like makes. The length is about 40'. Here are the maintenance records for the past five years, all up to date, no problems"

"I see you've done your homework."

"Yes, Daddy."

"I took her down the coast the other day with the owner. She handles beautifully and is very quiet."

"I don't see any reason why you shouldn't have it."

He reached in his desk and pulled out his checkbook and wrote in the full amount.

"Here you go sweetheart."

"Oh Daddy, you've made me so happy! Thank you, thank you."

She gave him a big hug and kiss on the cheek.

"You're welcome, honey."

CHAPTER 43

Alecia could not believe they reached Catalina in a little less than an hour. It looked beautiful. When they were about twenty minutes away from the island, dolphins accompanied them the rest of the way. When they arrived, they walked down main street and had a wonderful lunch at a place on the water. Jim told her about all the things they could do. They decided on the zip line first, then paragliding the next day.

After the zip line, they went to their hotel. It was beautiful. Everyone on the island was so friendly, visitors and locals. Alecia couldn't get over it. They decided to rest a little before dinner hour.

"Jim, this was such a great idea. I love this place."

"So do I, Alecia."

Jim was a considerate and passionate lover. Alecia could hardly wait for them to make love. They were laying close together on the bed. He reached for her.

"I can't seem to get enough of you, Alecia."

"I love everything you do to me, Jim. You are incredible."

"You are too, Alecia."

He pressed into her, his hardness growing. Alecia started to move her body against his and moaned softly. Wait a minute Alecia. Jim got up, closed the blinds, and put a do not disturb sign on their door. They started removing each other's clothes, quickly.

Catalina was known for its excellent restaurants. They chose a different one each night. The ocean all along main street was breathtaking. There was something so special and very romantic about dining on the water. They ordered a special champagne before dinner since this was their last night.

As they toasted, Jim said, "Alecia, I never realized how much I was missing until I met you."

Alecia became teary-eyed, "For both of us Jim."

They left Catalina the next day so Alecia could meet her parents at LAX in the afternoon with Sandy and Ramon.

Sandy was overcome when she saw Alecia's parents. It had been a long time since she had seen them. Almost fifteen years. They had literally saved Sandy from a miserable life in the foster homes. She owed them so much. They were her family and they felt the same way about her.

She had even gifted her boat to Alecia's son, Brian after Sandy married Ramon. She knew how much he loved boats and the water.

She started to tear up when she introduced Ramon.

"I want you to meet my husband, Ramon."

"Sandy has told me so many wonderful things about you and your husband. We are so glad you came. Our house is your house."

When they were all settled at Ramon and Sandy's, it didn't take long to catch up on everything. It was just like old times.

"Alecia, when can your father and I meet your new friend, Jim?"

"Tomorrow night at dinner. He is anxious to meet both of you too."

CHAPTER 44

The next evening, Sandy and Ramon had invited everyone for dinner at his parent's restaurant, La Puerta Abierta, The Open Door, in San Pedro. Ramon's parents, Roberto and Beatrice met them with open arms at the door. Introductions were made and they were led into the restaurant and seated close to the mariachi players.

Roberto made his signature margaritas for everyone and Beatrice brought out trays of her delicious appetizers. For dinner, Beatrice served all kinds of sumptuous Mexican food and her famous house enchilada specialty. Everything was superb. Everyone was having a great time. The mariachis started taking song requests.

"Senorita Alecia, what is your favorite song?"

"I love Cuando Cuando Cuando."

She and Jim got up and danced to it and the mariachi's played it several times.

They all stayed until closing time. No one really wanted to leave. They couldn't thank Roberto and Beatrice enough.

CHAPTER 45

It was early Saturday morning. Brian looked out his dorm window at USC at the sunshine and thought what a perfect day to study down at my boat. He could get some rays and a good tan, while studying. It was always quiet there with no interruptions. Brian loved his boat and was so grateful to Sandy for her generosity when she gifted it to him.

Brian was a junior at USC and studying hard for finals before his senior year. He was enjoying the warm rays of the sun on his boat until he heard a familiar voice.

"Hi there, stranger."

He looked up and saw Eva, his ex-girlfriend, standing on the boat next to his. She was in the skimpiest bikini he had ever seen.

"Hi, Eva. What brings you here?"

"I bought this boat, Brian, so I guess we are neighbors now."

Brian didn't know what to say. He suddenly felt nauseous. They had recently broken up after having a serious but tumultuous relationship for a couple of years.

"You'll have to excuse me. I've got a lot of studying to do today, so I better get busy. Congratulations on your boat, Eva!"

He turned and went down below deck to chase down a couple of aspirin with some beer. His head was beginning to throb.

He wondered how in the hell did this happen? And what made her do this? It was creeping him out. He felt like he was living in a fishbowl. And she was the man-eating fish. He didn't like this at all. He wished Jim Porter; the previous marina manager was still here. He might have been able to avoid this from happening. But Jim had retired and he and his mom, Alecia were an item now and were on a little trip. They would be back in a few more days.

Brian could hardly wait to break the news to his mom and also Jim. His mother had never cared for Eva. She felt she was too rich, very spoiled, and always got her way. The boat broker who sold the boat to Eva had no idea of the past relationship between Brian and Eva. When the broker saw Eva, he thought Brian would be pleased to have her as the new boat owner next to him, and the new marina manager who replaced Jim Porter thought the same.

Brian's mom called him right away when she and Jim returned from their trip.

"Hi sweetie, we're home. Hope everything is okay."

"Not really mom. I need to talk to you and Jim right

away."

"Why don't we take you to dinner tonight? How about 7:00 pm at your favorite Chinese restaurant? Sound good?"

"Sounds great mom, see you and Jim there."

Brian could hardly wait to tell them the latest.

When they were all at the restaurant, Brian said, "First, let's have drinks, and I want to hear about your trip, then I'll tell you what happened after dinner."

After they had eaten, they ordered after dinner drinks. Alecia and Jim were both anxious to hear what Brian had to say.

"Okay, you know Eva and I have broken up for good. You're not going to believe this. She bought the boat next to mine."

"You're kidding, Brian."

"No, I'm not, mom. It's creepy and doesn't make any sense."

Jim looked worried.

"This doesn't surprise me, Brian, with her mean disposition."

"I know, mom."

"It sounds like she might have become a stalker, Brian. In your boat documents that Sandy gave to you, you have something that lists all the rules and regulations the boat owners must adhere to. I can go over these with you. Then I think it would be a good idea for you to talk to Ramon and see what suggestions he has. You should also talk to the new marina manager and make him aware of the situation. I would like to be included in any way I can, Brian. If that's okay with you. I might be able to help."

"Absolutely. Thank you, Jim"

"I never realized Eva knew that much about boats, Brian."

"She sure does, mom. We took all the boat courses offered at the marina. She excelled in everything. She knows all about maintenance, can maneuver the boat like a pro and has no problem on the open sea, by herself."

When Brian told Ramon all the details, Ramon started shaking his head.

"What do you think, Ramon?"

"Sounds like she may have become a stalker, Brian."

"What can I do?"

"About all you can do right now is sit tight. However, if she starts bothering you, I want you to keep me informed. Keep a record of the date, day, time, and the problem, in detail. If I can justify a restraining order, we will put one on her. Unfortunately, that's about it for now."

"Thank you, Ramon."

"Be sure to keep me informed, Brian. I don't like the sound of this. These things usually have a way of getting pretty nasty."

"Will do."

"It's important to discuss the situation with the new boat manger so he can make his staff aware of all this too. But for now, let's be positive. Maybe she really misses being on a boat now that you're broken up."

"Let's hope so."

"Brian, whose idea was it to break up?"

"All mine, mom."

"What was her reaction?"

"She had one of her horrible screaming fits which only reinforced my decision to end the relationship."

"Good for you, Brian."

CHAPTER 46

At 9:00 am the lieutenant called a special department meeting.

"We have someone very special here with us today, that you all know. He is here to assist us in the disappearance of our three missing local ladies. He has helped us many times before and we are grateful he is here again to assist us. Please welcome Pauley O'Brian from the Valley office."

The department started cheering loudly and stomping their feet. Pauley's reputation preceded him. He knew how to get the job done and was the master of disguises. Because he was a great impersonator as a woman, he was perfect for the case of the missing ladies.

"Okay guys, quiet down. Pauley, come out and say hi to everyone."

No response.

"Pauley, are you there?"

Still no response.

"What the…"

The lieutenant caught a glimpse of Pauley back stage and then he got it. He raised his voice.

"PAULINE, if you are back there, please come out and say hi to everyone."

Suddenly a voluptuous blonde strode out in a sexy black dress. Pandemonium broke out. The department went crazy. They all stood and started chanting.

"Pauley, Pauley!"

They loved this guy. No one knew if he was gay or straight, it didn't matter. Pauley was a loner and always worked alone. He was one of the best and he was tough as nails. No one messed with Pauley.

"Okay everyone, help yourself to pastries and coffee. Pauley will join you in a few minutes after he changes into his regular clothes. You'll have about forty-five minutes to talk about old times, then I would like to see Pauley, Ramon, and Ted in my office at 10:30 to go over this case. As a reminder, if you should see Pauley in a dress be sure to address him as Pauline. We don't want to give away his cover."

At 10:30 am sharp, Pauley, Ramon, and Ted were in the lieutenant's office.

"Okay guys, let's talk about the missing women. First of all, let's go over the information Ramon and Ted have for you so far, Pauley. We know the ladies' similarities; where they lived, personal life, what bars they frequented, any trouble they were in, credit reports and so on. Anything else that comes to mind, Pauley?"

"Not at this time, lieutenant. I'm ready to start frequenting the places they went to and see if anything jumps out at me or anybody gets my attention."

"Okay, let's plan to meet next week at the same time in my office to review what we have."

The next morning, Pauley went over the information he had. All three women lived alone, they had blonde hair, ages were between 30-45, and they frequented the same bars alone, three in particular. Pauley noticed they all seemed to be heavy drinkers and only went to the bars in the evening, and stayed until they closed. Pauley started going to the three bars on a regular basis. He would stay until closing time at each bar to see if anything unusual developed. He wasn't getting any suspicious feelings about anyone until one night at the second bar. He caught the bartender, Al watching him. He went back to the same bar the next night to see if it happened again and was not just his imagination. It did.

Pauley was always fortunate enough to find a secluded table all to himself. He had a good view of everyone in the bar and they could also see him. There was usually a plant close by where he could water it with his drinks. He would put up the menu in front of him so no one could see what he was doing.

Pauley never had to pay for a drink himself. There was an endless supply of men that took care of that for him. They would always ask him for his phone number and if he would like to go out sometime. He noticed the bartender, Al, frequently staring at him. The next night when the bar was almost empty except for Pauley, Al came over to him.

"I'll be closing pretty soon. You've had quite a bit to drink. Do you think you'll be able to get home?"

"Sure, I can call a cab. I don't have a car."

Pauley could not only impersonate a woman, but he could alter his voice to sound like one, otherwise known as voice feminization. Pauley, slurring his words said.

"I want one more drink."

The bartender brought him another drink. After Pauley downed the last one, or so the bartender thought, he said, "I'm closing now."

Pauley pretended to stagger as he tried to stand up.

"Is your family close by?"

"No, there's just me."

"What's your name?"

"Pauline."

"My name is Al. Let's go. I'll take you home. It's hard to find a cab at this hour."

Al helped Pauline get into his truck. Pauley pushed the recording button on his special-made wrist watch.

"Tell me where you live."

Pauley gave him his motel address, which was close by. As they were driving, Pauley said, "This doesn't look like my neighborhood."

"Don't worry Pauline, I want to make a stop first."

They drove a few miles out of town and stopped in front of a secluded house which you could barely see behind the overgrown vegetation and weeds. It was old and needed a lot of work. Pauley acted like he was about to pass out. Al got him out of the truck and led him into his house. Pauley had noticed he had left his keys in the truck's ignition. Al took Pauley into the bedroom and sat him down on the bed.

"Make yourself comfortable, sweetie. You're going to love this."

Al wasted no time. He unzipped his pants and pushed himself on top of Pauley. Pauley pretended to resist. Al said, "Damn it. Hold still, you'll be begging for more. I'm going to hurt you if you don't do what I tell you. I like doing this. You better like it too, or you'll wind up like the others did."

"What do you mean?"

"Never you mind. That's my little secret. No one will

ever know. Just do what I tell you or you'll wind up just like the others."

"How was that?"

"You ask too many questions, girlie. Now shut up, I'm not going to warn you again."

At that point, Pauley felt he had enough information to get a conviction. His hands went around Al and he shoved him so hard he flew off Pauley and landed face down on the hard floor. Pauley jumped up and grabbed his coat nearby and took his cuffs out of the inside pocket. Al was still gasping for air and trying to get his breath. Pauley put his foot on his back and put Al's hands behind his back, cuffed him and read him his rights. He then hit the stop button on his watch to stop the recording. He yanked Al up and dragged him out to his truck and threw him in the passenger seat. He was glad the keys were still in the ignition. One less problem to deal with. Pauley got in the driver's side and started the engine. Still gasping for air, Al asked in a hoarse voice.

"Where are you taking me?"

"Where you belong you miserable piece of shit."

Pauley had no problem finding his way back to the police station. He had been in the area several times before to help out with other cases. It would take about twenty minutes.

When they reached the station, Pauley yanked him out of

the car and dragged him into the station. There were a couple of officers present as well as the desk clerk. They all shouted.

"Hi Pauline! What have you got for us?"

"A piece of garbage that needs to be processed."

After Al was processed and the jailor was taking him to his cell, the officers could overhear him say.

"Jesus, that is one tough broad."

The officers broke out laughing.

"That's our Pauley!"

Pauley switched back to his normal voice when Al, the bartender, was out of earshot.

"Okay guys, I need a couple of evidence bags for my dress and watch."

One of the officers spoke up.

"I'll get them for you, Pauley."

When he returned with them, Pauley thanked him.

"I can hardly wait to get out of my dress and take a shower. It's driving me crazy."

He looked down at his dress and completely lost it.

"God damn it, that asshole has ruined my dress."

The officers could not stop laughing.

"It was my favorite one, too."

"Don't worry Pauley, the department will get you a new one."

"I'm going to the locker room to shower and change into my regular clothes. I left them in one of the empty lockers."

He took the evidence bags with him and off he went.

When Pauley got to the locker room, he got out of his dress and put it in one evidence bag and his watch with the recording in the other. He stood in the steaming hot water for a good twenty minutes. It felt wonderful. He felt like a new person. Thank goodness his shoes were okay. Pauley always wore a pair of dressy black flats that he had made specifically to wear with his female disguises. He had a shiny buckle added to each shoe for a more feminine touch. They were perfect and very comfortable. He had to be able to move quickly when needed and could not be handicapped with high heels. He could never understand how women could wear those things. When he came out, the officers said, "Pauley, you look like a new man in more ways than one."

"Thank goodness. Can someone drive me back to the motel? I left my car over there."

"No problem, Pauley."

Before they left, Pauley logged in the evidence bags. When

they reached his motel, he thanked them for the ride.

"You bet, Pauley. Good to see you."

Pauley went into the motel restaurant. He was starving and ate a huge breakfast. When he returned to his room, it was about 9:00 am. He called the lieutenant and told him what happened.

"He's our guy, lieutenant. The recording on my watch should seal everything."

"Good work, Pauley. Why don't you come down to my office after you get some sleep? We can go over everything then. Does 2:00 pm sound okay?"

"That's perfect."

"Great work, Pauley."

"Thank you, lieutenant. See you soon."

Before Pauley dozed off, he thought I am so glad I caught that asshole before any more women disappeared. He felt very sad for the three women whose lives that monster had destroyed. He couldn't imagine what they went through and what he did with them.

Pauley got to the lieutenant's office right at 2:00 pm. The lieutenant waved him in.

"How's the interrogation going so far lieutenant?"

"Pretty good. He's not going to lawyer up so that's a

plus. I think we can eventually get him to tell us what he did with the bodies."

"I sure hope so, lieutenant."

The lieutenant chuckled.

"What lieutenant?"

"I heard he ruined your dress."

"That was my favorite one, too. Oh well, it wasn't my best color anyway."

They both started laughing.

"You know, lieutenant, I'll never live that one down."

"That's okay Pauley, because you're their favorite. You're tough and you know how to get the job done."

"Thank you, lieutenant."

When the lieutenant heard the recording on Pauley's watch he was knocked out. He knew they could get a conviction.

"You did a great job for us, Pauley."

"Thank you, lieutenant. I'm glad to be of help any time."

It was getting close to 5:00 pm.

"Pauley, I think we need to celebrate. I'm going to take you to a restaurant that has the best steaks and drinks in town. How does that sound?"

"Terrific, lieutenant. I'm ready."

CHAPTER 47

Sandy and Ramon's house looked beautiful for their holiday Christmas party. When Jim Porter arrived, he spotted Alecia with her parents right away. After introductions were made, Jim asked them.

"Can I get you folks something to drink and a few appetizers?"

Alecia's father said, "That sounds great, Jim."

Alecia said, "I'll help you, Jim."

He and Alecia went over to the bar.

"Where's Brian?"

"He's around here somewhere."

Everyone seemed to be drinking champagne, so Jim took some for themselves and her parents.

"I'll get us some more appetizers, Alecia."

They found a place where they could all chat easily. Jim enjoyed talking to her parents immensely but couldn't keep his eyes off Alecia.

They spent the next two hours chatting and then Brian came and joined in the conversation. Sandy kept an eye on Alecia and Jim. She could tell how attracted they were to each other.

Blitz and Angelina even joined in the holiday festivities. Donna and Stephen were in the den, enjoying Blitz and Angelina. They couldn't get over how inseparable they were. After all of the attention, Blitz jumped in his bed followed by Angelina. Blitz was very careful to not squash her in their bed. She curled up in Blitz's thick coat, especially his neck. Once in a while her purring was interrupted and you could see her bright green eye peeking out at everyone. Ted and Janet Siciliano joined them. They were just as amazed as Stephen and Donna. Angelina was ignoring Ted and giving all her attention to Blitz.

Ted said, in his strongest Italian accent, "Angelina, have you forgotten who brought you here?"

He liked to remind Angelina that he was responsible for her being here.

Ted was very proud of Angelina's Italian heritage, and his own. Ted and his wife, Janet, were so happy they had given Angelina as a wedding present to Sandy and Ramon.

Stephen said, "Ramon, what a sight. Are you sure Blitz knows he's in the K-9 unit?"

"Just look at that 1st place trophy on the mantle, lieutenant, and 1st place in his graduating class."

The Christmas party was a great success and ended very late. Everyone was having such a good time, they were reluctant to leave.

CHAPTER 48

Since Raymond Martin was arrested in California for a murder he committed in Arizona, he was transferred back to Arizona to be tried. He was very lucky he was in one of Arizona's more lenient prisons. It seemed that most of the prisons in Arizona had become overcrowded.

He was in the prison cafeteria drinking his last cup of coffee after breakfast to the last drop. Just as he got up to leave, he saw a group of prisoners being led outside to board a bus. He remembered a group of them were being transferred to another prison which had more room. They seemed to be in a hurry and were probably behind schedule. Raymond quickly saw an opening and merged in with the group and boarded the bus. He fit right in. They were all dressed in denim shirts and pants which had recently been issued to everyone replacing their worn-out older uniforms. They took off right away.

The prison they were moving the prisoners to was about fifty miles away. About halfway there they had a flat tire. Because of the intense heat, the prisoners were removed from the bus. They were in a heavily wooded area with a lot of shade which was a lot cooler. As the tire was being replaced, Raymond ducked quickly behind a large tree.

Raymond crept away staying close to the heavily wooded area. He finally came to a road and followed it hoping he would eventually run into civilization. After walking a few miles, he spotted a building in the distance. As he got closer, he saw it was a farm and saw somebody working outside. The farmer saw him coming and Raymond gave a friendly wave. When he got closer, he said, "Howdy. It's nice to see a friendly face."

The farmer smiled. He was a big rugged looking guy. Raymond noticed he was wearing a holstered pistol. He didn't want to mess with this guy. He could obviously take care of himself. He explained to the farmer his car had been stolen and he was trying to reach the closest town. They talked for a while over a cup of coffee.

"Maybe I can help you. I can drive you to the closest town."

"Thank you, that would be great."

They got in his truck and took off. The town was about half an hour away.

"Here we are. Do you have any money?"

"No, he took my wallet too."

"You're lucky to be alive. I've been in that situation myself. Here's fifty bucks to help you out. Don't worry about paying me back."

Raymond couldn't thank him enough and got out of the truck.

The town was fairly large. Raymond went to the nearest diner and ate a huge meal. The server told him tour buses stopped there on a regular basis. One should be coming in pretty soon. After eating, Raymond went to a small concession stand and bought a few small items.

Right on schedule, a bus came roaring in. Raymond purchased a ticket and got on the bus. He dropped something in a nearby mailbox before he got on the bus.

A few days later, Ramon received an envelope addressed to him from Arizona. Curious, he opened it. There was a note that simply read:

> "I told you I was smart."

CHAPTER 49

Ivan was sick and tired of apartment living and had been looking to buy a house for some time. He had his eye on Ed Miller's place in San Pedro. It was a charming, small house in a great neighborhood. He and Ed had been good friends for some time. Ed was getting pretty old and told Ivan if he ever decided to sell, he hoped Ivan would be the buyer. Ivan hoped so too. One afternoon, as Ivan was cruising on his bike, he went by Ed's place and spotted him outside and waved. Ed motioned him over.

"How ya doing, Ivan?"

"Great Ed, how about you?"

"I'm good. Ivan, can you come in for a few minutes? I need to talk to you."

"Sure, Ed."

"Sit down and I'll pour us some coffee."

"Sounds good."

"Ivan, my kids are pressuring me to sell and move up to Washington to be closer to them. I'm thinking it's a pretty good idea. You know I'm getting up there. Do you still want to buy my home?"

"I sure do!"

"I've been doing some research."

He gave Ivan a piece of paper.

"I think this is a fair price. What do you think, Ivan?"

"Looks fair to me, Ed."

Ivan knew the house inside and out. His biker guys always took care of any work that Ed needed to have done. The house was in excellent shape and condition.

"I would like a quick escrow, Ivan."

"How about 30 days or less, Ed?"

"Let's do it, Ivan. My family will be very pleased."

Ivan had a great relationship with his banker and knew there would be no problem with financing.

"I'll get the ball rolling, contact Mary at escrow and get that started, Ivan."

Ivan took out his check book.

"I'm going to give you a good faith non-refundable deposit right now, Ed."

"That's not necessary, Ivan."

"I know, but I feel better about doing it."

CHAPTER 50

The escrow went smoothly and quickly, and they closed in a little less than thirty days. Ivan moved in immediately and Ed left for Washington to be with his family.

Ivan loved the place. He started making some changes. He called a landscaper he knew at the local nursery and told him about the changes he would like him to make.

"Please remove any grass in front and replace it with a variation of low maintenance succulents and palm plants."

The back patio was perfect. It was extra-large and bricked in nicely. It was perfect for entertaining.

Ivan had one group of bikers put in a large fire pit in the center of the patio. Ivan then ordered stone bench seating with backs put around the firepit. Darlene helped him pick out colorful cushions for comfortable seating.

Ivan thought the benches would be perfect for his bikers with their enormous weight and size which averaged 300lbs to 6'5" in height, even though the stone benches were pricey, Ivan thought overall they were a good investment. At least he wouldn't have to be replacing capsized patio chairs from his oversized bikers on a regular basis.

Another group of bikers built an attractive bar. Darlene picked out a colorful awning to protect the bar in case of bad weather. Close to the bar there was another area for eating and drinking. A nice, elongated stone table was ordered with a long stone bench completely covered by a cushion for comfort.

Ivan was beside himself.

He shouted, "Great work guys!"

Everything was shaping up nicely. All he had left to do was purchase a large high-end barbeque and have the patio decorated with beautiful lights. He could hardly wait to have his housewarming party for his bikers and close friends.

CHAPTER 51

Donna and Stephen were sharing the newspaper at breakfast one morning. Suddenly Donna tore out an entire page of the paper.

"Honey, did you see this?"

"What is it?"

LOS ANGELES COUNTY CONTEST

$100,000 TO BE AWARDED TO THE MOST OUSTANDING CITIZEN FOR HIS/HER CONTRIBUTIONS TO THEIR COMMUNITY.

The winner will be honored at a special dinner given at the White House by President Moyer. A complimentary three-day hotel stay is included at the
Hay-Adams Hotel.

"You know who I'm thinking of Stephen?"

"I certainly do, Ivan."

"Just look at all he does and continues to do."

"It seems like everything he does benefits the community in some way."

"You know he has been influential in the renovation of commercial properties and underdeveloped areas."

"Look at how he renovated my buildings. My apartments look like new. I'm getting top rents and there are no vacancies."

"Look at all the crimes he has helped you solve."

"He has been instrumental in eliminating the drug gangs in the harbor area. Now businesses feel safe and have reopened."

"He has created a twenty-man biker group that helps the community with anything from handyman problems to complex construction projects. And the list just goes on and on."

"Stephen, I have never known anyone in my lifetime that has helped so many in the community, have you?"

"None even come close, sweetheart."

"Let's put something together and enter him. I'll have everything typed up and submitted right away."

"It says all submittals must be received within the next thirty days. The winner will be announced thirty days after the submitted cutoff date."

"Oh Stephen, I am so excited. Remind me to use Ivan's new address on the form. He's moved in his house now. It's looking really nice and I can hardly wait until he has his house warming party."

CHAPTER 52

Ivan had been in his house a little over a month. One day as he was coming home from work, he saw FedEx parked in front of his house.

"Hi Sam. How's it going? Have you got something for me?"

"I sure do, Ivan. Something very special."

"Really?"

"Yep, look at this."

He handed Ivan a large, thick white envelope. Everything was embossed in gold. The return address read The White House.

"I've never delivered one of these before, Ivan."

Ivan opened the envelope slowly. His hands were shaking a little.

"What is it, Ivan?"

"I'm not sure, Sam. I've got to sit down and read all this. I'll let you know the details later."

"I understand, Ivan."

CHAPTER 53

Ivan went inside his house to read the invitation. He felt a little dizzy and sat down in his most comfortable chair.

CONGRATULATIONS

You have won the Los Angeles County Contest for the most outstanding citizen for contributing to your community. You will be honored at a special dinner given by President Moyer at the White House. $100,000 will be awarded to you at the dinner. This includes a complimentary three-day stay at the Hay-Adams Hotel for you and your guest.

Ivan read and re-read the invitation. A White House staff member would be at his house next Friday at 9:00 am to take him and his guest to the Van Nuys Airport to board a White House Gulfstream plane for Washington D.C. On arrival at the capitol, they would be taken to the Hay-Adams Hotel for a complimentary three day stay.

At 6:30 pm that same day, they would be escorted to the White House to meet President Moyer. Festivities would begin with a cocktail party and a dinner at the White House with the president and other guests. The next two days are at your leisure.

The day following the two leisure days, you will depart in one of our Gulfstreams at 9:00 am to return home. Upon your arrival at the Van Nuys Airport, another staff member will meet you and take you and your guest to your homes.

An RSVP is requested, and a contact number was given. Ivan sat there in shock for a full ten minutes. This was incredible. How did this even happen? He had a feeling Donna and Stephen had something to do with this.

He would RSVP, then he would call Darlene and take her to a special dinner tonight to surprise her with the news, and then call Donna and Stephen to tell them.

CHAPTER 54

Ivan's first priority was to get his man-bun removed. It just didn't seem appropriate for the White House. He and Ramon had lots of hair. It was very thick and black and naturally curly. He called the young lady who did Ramon's hair and made an appointment. It was a very small, but professional looking shop. When Ivan walked in a very pretty girl said, "Hi there, you must be Ivan."

"Yes I am."

"I'm Sue."

She sat him down in her chair.

"Any special requests today?"

"Yes, please get rid of my man-bun."

"Good, let's get you to the shampoo bowl."

Sue started shampooing then massaging Ivan's neck. It felt wonderful. No wonder Ramon came to her.

"You've got great hair, Ivan."

"Thank you."

Ivan was there for a good hour.

"Are you doing this for anyone special, Ivan?"

"Yes, I guess I am. I have a date with the president."

She thought, 'Sure you do', and answered politely, "Of course, of course. Well, you're going to look fantastic when I'm done."

When Ivan left, he felt like a new person. He also noticed the opposite sex kept giving him the once over. It made him feel good.

CHAPTER 55

Ivan still couldn't believe it. He called Darlene. She would be off work by now.

"Darlene, I have a big surprise for you. I'll pick you up at 7:00 pm for a special dinner. We're going to celebrate."

"What is it, Ivan?"

"I'll tell you over drinks when we get there. You won't believe it!"

When Ivan picked her up, she cried, "Good grief, your man-bun is gone! You're absolutely gorgeous."

Ivan beamed.

Ivan took Darlene to the best restaurant in San Pedro overlooking the harbor. When Darlene saw where they were going, she said, "Ivan, I'm on pins and needles. This must be some surprise!"

"I'll tell you over our drinks."

They ordered their favorite drinks, martinis, and Ivan handed her the white envelope. Darlene read it, her eyes wide, then re-read it with her mouth open.

"Ivan, this is unbelievable. How did this happen?"

"I think Donna and Stephen may have had something to do with this."

"I hope you can be excused from work."

"I'll tell my boss right away."

"Where will we be staying, Ivan?"

"At the Hay-Adams Hotel. I understand it's right across the street from the White House."

First thing in the morning, Darlene asked her boss if she could take a few days off. When she told him why, he was so excited for her, "Of course, Darlene. I'll even take your place while you're gone. This kind of thing only happens once in a lifetime, if at all."

Darlene let Ivan know right away.

CHAPTER 56

When Ivan called Donna, he heard her scream.

"OH MY GOD, STEPHEN, IVAN WON THE CONTEST! HE WON, HE WON, HE WON! We want to hear all about it. Can you come over tonight, Ivan?"

"Sure thing."

"6:00 pm would be great. Stephen will be home from work by then. I'll order a pizza and Italian food for dinner."

CHAPTER 57

The first thing Donna noticed when Ivan arrived was his hair.

"Wow, you look terrific, Ivan without that damn man-bun."

"Thank you, Donna."

Ivan took everything he had received from the White House for Donna and Stephen to see. They sat with their open mouths, completely overcome.

"I have a feeling you two might have been responsible for this."

Donna and Stephen looked very sheepishly.

"You deserved this more than anyone, Ivan. It was our pleasure. We are so happy for you."

"Well, I can't thank you both enough."

"We just want to hear all about your trip from the beginning to end when you return."

CHAPTER 58

It was time to leave for the Capitol. The staff member for the White House was at Ivan's house at 9:00 am sharp. When they reached the airport location for private planes at the Van Nuys Airport, Darlene gasped.

"Ivan, is that the plane we are going on?"

"I think so, Darlene."

"Good grief, it's enormous. I hope it can get off the ground."

"Don't worry, Darlene, it will."

Their luggage was loaded and the steward showed them to their seats.

"When we are at cruising altitude sir, I will serve you and your guest breakfast."

He gave them a menu to select from.

"Ivan, I think this plane is bigger than my apartment."

"Could be, Darlene. I know it has everything. The living room we are seated in, bar, bedroom, bathroom with shower, and kitchen."

"Unbelievable."

CHAPTER 59

Their flight was wonderful. They felt like they were floating on air and landed in Washington D.C. in no time.

A staff member greeted them as they departed the plane.

"Good afternoon, sir. Let me get your luggage and I'll take you to your hotel, the Hay-Adams."

They were ushered to their suite. Ivan and Darlene couldn't believe it. Their suite was beautiful and very large.

"Do you need me to unpack for you sir or press anything for you?"

"We're fine. Thank you."

As they were hanging up their clothes, their door buzzed and Ivan opened the door. An attendant in a white jacket stood with a cart carrying an ice bucket with champagne, beluga caviar with wafers and assorted crackers, and other delicious appetizers.

"Compliments of President Moyer, sir. Congratulations. You've become a celebrity here. I wish we had someone like you in the community where I live."

Ivan turned beet red.

"Thank you."

"The President thought you might want to relax a little after your flight. The champagne is a favorite of his. Please enjoy."

Ivan gave him a generous tip.

"Oh, before you leave, could you take a few photos of us in front of the window with the White House in the background?"

"Of course, sir."

Ivan and Darlene toasted each other with the champagne.

"Let's give this a try, Darlene. What do you think?"

"It certainly beats our drinks at home. I think I could get used to this kind of life very quickly, Ivan."

"Me too. By the way, what time do we leave for the White House tonight and how do we get there?"

"A car will be waiting for us outside the hotel at 6:00 pm."

At 6:00 pm a staff member was waiting for them in the lobby of the Hay-Adams. He drove them across the street to the White House where they were escorted in. Ivan felt everything was surreal. They were put in a waiting room.

"The President will be with you shortly."

In a few minutes, a door opened and in came President Moyer.

"I'm so glad to meet you, Ivan and Darlene. I hope your flight was pleasant?"

"Yes, sir. Thank you, Mr. President."

"Come, let's join the others at your cocktail party. Everybody is anxious to meet you."

There were about twenty-five other guests having cocktails. Mostly men and a few women. Ivan recognized several of them which were on the Gulfstream with them. Everyone was very anxious to meet and talk with Ivan. An hour later, they all went in to sit down for dinner. The President spoke about Ivan's extraordinary contributions to his community. Everyone applauded and toasted him with champagne.

After dinner, the President awarded Ivan with a check for $100,000. Ivan almost fell out of his chair. He had forgotten all about the prize money. The other guests gave Ivan their business cards and asked for his email so they could remain in touch. The party was a great success. Ivan and Darlene were returned to their hotel sometime after midnight.

CHAPTER 60

"That was some party, wasn't it, Darlene?"

"It certainly was. You're a good man, Ivan. That's what I love about you."

"Thank you, Darlene."

"Do we have anything to drink? I need to relax a little."

"This looks good, Ivan."

"Let's try it."

"Mmmmm. This is good. Very smooth, some kind of liquor."

"Darlene, this feels like some kind of dream, doesn't it? You looked so beautiful tonight. I think I would like to ravish you."

"Maybe we should ravish each other, Ivan."

And they did.

CHAPTER 61

The next morning President Moyer called Ivan at the Hay-Adams.

"Good morning Ivan. I can't tell you how much I and my other guests enjoyed your company last night. You were very impressive and I'm sure you will hear from them in the future. I may call upon you myself now and then. Please give my best to Darlene. She added so much spark with her wonderful personality and sense of humor. We hope you both enjoyed your stay with us just as much as we enjoyed having both of you."

"We certainly did, Mr. President."

"Enjoy your days of leisure in our city and have a safe trip home."

"Remember, you are always welcome."

"Thank you, Mr. President."

CHAPTER 62

During their two days of leisure, Ivan and Darlene took in as many sights as they could. At night, they enjoyed going to clubs to hear some music which had been recommended to them at the White House party.

The next day as they were checking out of the Hay-Adams, Ivan spoke to the manager.

"We thoroughly enjoyed our stay here. Your hotel is very beautiful and the service we received was excellent."

"We hope you come back again soon. You are always welcome."

"Thank you, sir. I would like to gift my best friends a special stay here soon."

"When you know when they will be coming, please let me know." He gave Ivan his business card. "I will personally take good care of them."

"Thank you, sir."

"Have a safe trip home."

CHAPTER 63

Their dream had come to an end as they boarded the Gulfstream at 9:00 am to return home. But Ivan and Darlene would never forget it. They would always have their beautiful memories to treasure forever.

CHAPTER 64

Jim and Alecia decided to spend New Year's Eve at their favorite Italian restaurant, Giovanni's. It had now become Alecia's favorite restaurant, as well as Jim's. Giovanni greeted them with open arms and escorted them to their special table. He brought over his complimentary assortment of appetizers for them and a bottle of a very fine Italian Prosecco wine to bring in the New Year. They toasted and asked Giovanni to join them in a toast. They had a wonderful dinner followed by a very good after dinner liqueur that Giovanni wanted them to try. Afterward, Jim became more serious.

"I don't want you to go, Alecia. I want you to stay here permanently with me in my home. Please don't go."

"I feel the same way, Jim."

"I'm ready to retire now, Alecia. We can just enjoy each other on my retirement money."

Alecia was getting teary eyed.

"You know Alecia, most people never have in a lifetime what we have."

"I know, Jim. I know."

"Alecia, I can see your whole family moving here soon. Brian loves it here and has no intention of leaving after he graduates. Eventually your parents will be here too."

"I completely agree with you, Jim. But I think it would be better if I returned with my parents and explained everything to them when we are at home. Also, I would like to explain to my employer everything that has happened. They have been very good to me over the years."

"You're probably right, Alecia. How soon do you think you could return?"

"How about on Valentine's Day? Does that sound okay to you?"

"Yes."

"Jim, I'm still worried about Brian. Eva has such a mean streak and can be very vindictive. Brian's getting ready to go into his senior year at USC. He doesn't need a problem like this. You have to admit it does seem like Eva is stalking him. Why else would she buy that boat right next to his?"

"I have to agree with you, sweetheart. We will keep an eye out for any trouble while you're away. I'll talk to the new marina manager about the situation and he will alert his staff right away."

"Thank you, Jim. I know I can depend on you."

CHAPTER 65

The time for the Bowers family to return home came quickly. Everyone said their farewells teary eyed, and all the passengers started to board the plane.

"I can't wait to be back with you, Jim."

"Is there any special place you would like to go for Valentine's Day?"

"Yes, there is."

"Where is that, sweetheart?"

"Back to Catalina."

Jim smiled, "Our favorite."

Before Alecia boarded the plane, she and Jim held each other tightly and he whispered in her ear, "Hurry back, my Sweet Valentine."

And then she was gone.

CHAPTER 66

The first thing Jim did after leaving the airport was to go to the marina and see Bob Collins, the new manager who replaced him. He saw Bob in his office and went in.

"Hi Bob, do you have a few minutes?"

"Always for you, Jim. What's up?"

Jim explained the potential problem with Eva who had just purchased the boat next to Brian's.

"I had no idea of their prior relationship and the problems they were having, Jim. I am so glad you told me."

"We hope this isn't the case Bob, but Brian, his family, and Ramon at the LAPD who you know think she may be stalking Brian, and I tend to agree with them."

"I'll inform my staff right away Jim, and we will be on the alert for any trouble."

"Thank you, Bob. Please call Ramon if you notice anything unusual."

"Will do. Sorry this had to happen to Brian. He's a nice kid."

"He sure is."

CHAPTER 67

Lieutenant McClary called a special morning meeting for his staff.

"I called this meeting to introduce a newcomer to our homicide division. Please welcome detective Stephanie Green from one of our Northern California homicide divisions."

When Stephanie Green came out, everyone's mouth dropped open. She was a knockout with long thick black hair and the greenest eyes. She was about twenty-four with an outstanding reputation that preceded her. Her parents lived in Los Angeles, and she had always wanted to relocate to be closer to them. When the opportunity arose, she decided to take advantage of it.

CHAPTER 68

During dinner hour that night, Ramon was telling Sandy about Stephanie.

"Ramon, do me a favor and be sure Ivan invites her to his housewarming party. That will give her a chance to meet everyone."

"Good idea, Sandy."

Sandy, ever the matchmaker, knew Alecia's son, Brian, was coming to the party. Ramon could read her mind.

"Sweetheart, she's a few years older than Brian."

"That's okay, Ramon. You know age is just a number."

"Since he and Eva broke up, he might even bring a date."

Sandy called Brian right away.

"Brain, you could be a big help to Ivan at his party."

"How can I help?"

"There is a new female detective that has transferred

into the homicide division. She is from Northern California and her name is Stephanie Green."

"And?"

"Please arrive a little early so I can introduce you to her when she arrives. If you could make her feel at ease and introduce her to some of the guests, that would be great."

"Sure, I would be more than happy to do that. By the way, what does she look like?"

"Believe me Brain, you won't be disappointed. Trust me, don't bring a date to the party."

"Okay, Sandy."

CHAPTER 69

Alecia was still busy in Northern California planning on what she wanted to take to Jim's house in San Pedro since they were going to be living together. They talked every day on the phone.

"Hi sweetie, how are you doing with everything?"

"Pretty good. My parents are so happy for us Jim. They are crazy about you. What's happening there?"

"Not much."

"How's Eva?"

"No problem so far."

"That's surprising. I have a great idea. I'm going to drive up there tomorrow to help you pack. I'm sure everything will fit in my van perfectly and it will be much cheaper than shipping everything. What do you think?"

"I think it's a great idea and can hardly wait to see you."

"Oh, and we should be back here in time for Ivan's party. I'll leave early tomorrow morning and should be there sometime late in the afternoon."

"Drive safely, Jim. Not too fast. I love you so much. See you soon."

"Love you more sweetheart. Bye."

"Bye."

CHAPTER 70

Ivan's housewarming party included twenty of his biker buddies and fifteen of his closest friends. He figured with their dates and spouses, that would bring the total close to seventy. He was glad his patio could handle that many guests comfortably.

Ivan had everything catered for his party from Ramon's parent's, Roberto and Beatrice's, Mexican restaurant, La Puerta Abierta (The Open Door). Roberto was in charge of the bar with his signature margaritas, and he had brought one of his bartenders there to help him. Beatrice had brought two of their other employees to help her serve everything from her delicious appetizers to her wonderful specialty Mexican enchiladas. The aromas from her cooking were intoxicating. The mariachi players were scheduled to arrive later.

Brian arrived a little early as promised and met Sandy.

"I see Stephanie coming in now, Brian. Let's go meet her."

Brian was knocked out when he saw Stephanie. He was mesmerized by her beautiful green eyes. She was absolutely gorgeous. Sandy introduced them.

"Stephanie, I'm going to leave you with Brian who will take good care of you and introduce you to the other guests."

"Thank you, Sandy."

Brian's charm took over and he made Stephanie feel at ease immediately. To be polite, he decided to mingle with the other guests so she could meet more of them. With that out of the way, he could hardly wait to find a quiet place where he and Stephanie could get to know each other. He finally spotted a secluded spot where they could have some privacy.

"Stephanie let's take a break and sit down over there. Are you hungry?"

"As a matter of fact, I am and I love Mexican food."

"Great. I will get us a little bit of everything and also some margaritas."

Brian made several trips to get everything.

"This is delicious, Brian."

"I think this is the best Mexican food ever, Stephanie."

They talked about everything and enjoyed each other's company for the next couple of hours. The mariachi players arrived and began playing non-stop. Everyone started singing and some got up to dance.

"Stephanie, would you like to dance?"

"Sure."

They both loved dancing and danced the night away to the wonderful rhythm and beat of the mariachi music. Ivan's home-warming party was a huge success in more ways than one.

Sandy kept glancing over at Brian and Stephanie whenever she had the chance. She could tell they were having a great time together.

Brian did not want the evening to end without making a date to see Stephanie soon.

"Stephanie, when do you start work?"

"I have a week to relax."

"Could I interest you in doing some fun things?"

"I think I would like that, Brian."

"Why don't I call you tomorrow and we can set some things up."

"Here is my phone number, Brian."

"Great."

Brian saw his mom and Jim walking over.

"Stephanie, I would like you to meet my mother, Alecia, and her friend, Jim."

Alecia liked Stephanie right away. Who wouldn't? She was polite and couldn't be any nicer. She thought, finally my son has found someone special.

It didn't take long for Brian and Stephanie to start seeing each other. Brian took her to his boat and they liked to spend the night there frequently. He even made it a point to introduce her to Eva and get that out of the way as soon as possible.

CHAPTER 71

It was Friday afternoon.

"Steph, what would you like to do this weekend?"

"I don't know Brian. It would be nice to just relax for a couple of days before going to work."

"We could stay all night on my boat tonight and we could decide in the morning."

"That sounds like a plan."

"I do have to meet with my counselor at USC late this afternoon to go over my schedule for my senior year. I could be at the boat around 6:30 or 7."

"That will work for me, Brian. I can go down to the boat earlier and go over some of my upcoming cases."

"Perfect, I'll see you then."

Stephanie loved being on Brian's boat and found it quite relaxing as long as it was docked at the marina. Stephanie was definitely not a water person.

The weather appeared to be getting darker and darker. It looked like a storm was brewing. Red flags went up at the marina, warning boaters of a bad storm approaching. Boaters were advised to keep their boats securely docked in the marina.

As Stephanie was reviewing some of her open cases on Brian's boat, she must have dozed off from the gentle rocking motion of the boat. Suddenly, she woke up. The rocking motion had become much more intense.

She went up on deck to see what was happening. She froze. She could no longer see land, only a vast ocean surrounding her. She had never felt so alone. She called Brian, but his cell was turned off. He probably forgot to turn it back on after his meeting. Trying not to panic, she called Ramon and told him her situation.

"Ramon, I have no idea how this happened."

"Stephanie, remain calm. I'm calling the Coast Guard now and will get right back to you."

CHAPTER 72

Lieutenant McClary was worried sick about his new homicide detective Stephanie Green. The thought of her being stranded in the middle of the ocean in a nasty storm was overwhelming. He couldn't imagine what she was going through. The lieutenant was in constant communication with Ramon checking on her status. He and Ramon had a strong suspicion that Eva Peters was somehow involved. Ramon went to pick Eva up for questioning at the police station. She was definitely a prime suspect.

Brian's meeting was over and he was on his way to his boat. The weather had gotten much worse and it looked like they might be in for a very bad storm. He was thinking that maybe he had been too judgmental about Eva being a stalker. So far, since he and Stephanie had become more involved, Eva had been fine and had not been a problem. As Brian hurried down the gang plank to his boat, he stopped dead in his tracks. Where in the hell was his boat with Stephanie? He felt nauseous. He grabbed his cell to call her. Damn, he had forgotten to turn it back on. He saw he had a ton of new messages. Frantic, he called Stephanie's cell. Thank god she answered.

"Steph, what happened? Where are you?"

"I'm somewhere in the middle of the ocean in a bad storm. When I couldn't reach you, I called Ramon and he called the Coast Guard. They have a helicopter and vessel searching for me now."

"Brian, I have no idea how this happened."

"Have you talked to the Coast Guard?"

"Yes. They called my cell after Ramon called them and talked me through using the boat's radio. So, I'm okay there. I also have been sending flares up. I'm glad you have a lot of them."

"You know where my engine key is?"

"I do. The Coast Guard said they would need that."

"Brian, I hear the Coast Guard on the radio now. I have to go."

"Okay Stephanie, this is the radio operator again. I want you to send up some more flares, every fifteen minutes."

"When we have your location, our copter will fly over your boat and turn a bright spotlight on the boat's deck. One of our men will come down a ladder from our copter and drop onto the deck. He will take over the boat and bring you back to the marina. Our vessel will follow to make sure you arrive safely. Any questions?"

"No sir. I will be very happy when you reach me."

The ocean was becoming rougher and rougher. Twenty minutes went by. It seemed like an eternity. Stephanie sent up more flares.

On board the copter, the radio operator was getting worried.

"Captain, I hope we reach her soon. This storm is coming in faster than expected."

"I know, I know."

Time kept slipping away. Stephanie was getting more worried.

"Where are they?"

All of a sudden, a small blip appeared on the radar operator's electronic screen.

"Captain, we may have something."

"Stephanie, send up a couple more flares now."

More blips appeared.

"I've got her, Captain!"

"Stephanie, we've got you and we are on our way. We should reach you in ten to fifteen minutes."

Stephanie kept checking her watch. They should be here by now. Suddenly she thought she heard a faint whirring noise. It became louder. A bright spotlight lit up the deck.

The copter dropped a ladder.

"Ready Mitch? Be careful, the wind has really picked up. We'll flash the red light for you the minute you are over the deck."

"Got it."

Stephanie could see a man descending the ladder. The wind was furiously blowing the ladder in all directions like crazy. She saw a red light come on and a man dropped to the deck. He hit hard trying to keep his balance with the rocking and rolling of the boat. Stephanie ran to him to make sure he was okay. He smiled up at her.

"Hi pretty lady, you must be Stephanie. I'm Mitch Grant."

She felt like hugging and kissing him. He gave the high sign to the copter that he was okay.

"Ok Stephanie, I'm going to escort you safely back to your marina. Our Coast Guard vessel will follow us until they know we are safely there. Have you got an engine key for me?"

"I do. I'm sure glad to see you, Mitch."

She handed him the key. He was captivated by her green eyes. They reminded him of shiny emeralds.

"Let's get this baby started."

He put the key in the ignition and turned it. The engine coughed and sputtered, then dead silence. He tried again.

Same thing. Stephanie was praying, oh please, please start. Mitch turned the key hard again. VROOM the engine caught loud and clear.

"Third time works like a charm Stephanie. We are on our way. It should take us about thirty minutes. If you don't mind me asking, how did this happen to you?"

"I have no idea, Mitch. Maybe somebody was trying to get rid of me, permanently. Thanks to you and your colleagues, they didn't succeed."

"All in a days work, Stephanie. We are just glad you're okay. I have to hand it to you, you remained very calm through all this. What do you do?"

"I'm a homicide detective."

"Aha, that explains it."

"But I'm not a big lover of water. I only feel comfortable on a boat when it's docked on land. So, I'm not as brave as you think I am."

"Well, you did just fine."

"Thank you."

"Most people would have been terrified going through what you just went through. Is this your boat?"

"No, a good friend's."

"Boyfriend?"

"Yes, he's waiting for me at the marina."

She heard Mitch mumble, "Lucky guy".

Even though Mitch was drenched, Stephanie couldn't help noticing how handsome and muscular he was. He was very tall with thick black hair and penetrating brown eyes.

Every time he touched her or caught her when they hit a rough wave she could feel her desire for him bubbling up in her. She had a feeling he did too.

"We should reach your marina pretty soon now."

The storm was getting worse by the minute and the waves were starting to come over into the boat.

"It's pretty rough now Stephanie, but we are almost there."

All of a sudden Mitch pointed ahead, "Look Steph, I can make out some lights ahead, we're getting close to your marina."

"Stephanie, look, there's your marina up ahead."

As they got closer to shore, she could see Brian standing on the dock waiting for her.

"Is that your friend?"

"Yes, it is."

"Wait a minute, now I see two other guys? Do I have more competition?"

She laughed, "No, no. I think they are my superiors from work."

"Remember Stephanie, if your situation should ever change, you know how to reach me."

"Yes, I do. I can't thank you enough, Mitch. God knows what would have happened to me."

"I'm just so glad I could be of help to you."

His lips brushed gently across her mouth as he leaned down to give her a big hug and kiss on the cheek.

"I hope we meet again, Stephanie, under much better circumstances." She thought, 'So do I Mitch, so do I.'

Stephanie could feel the desire for him again. This is crazy, she thought. It must be the circumstances. She wanted more of him.

When they docked, Mitch helped Stephanie off the boat. She was still a bit shaky. Brian hugged and kissed her.

"Boy, am I glad to see you! Thank goodness you're safe."

He turned to Mitch.

"Thank you for getting my girl and my boat back safely."

"You're welcome."

The lieutenant and Ramon also gave her a big hug. Stephanie made all the proper introductions.

"Stephanie, after all you've been through, please take a few days off before coming back to work."

"Thank you, lieutenant."

When everyone said their goodbyes and started to leave, Stephanie blurted out.

"Mitch, can I give you a lift?"

"Thank you, Stephanie, but I have a car waiting for me."

He pointed to the car a short distance away.

Stephanie couldn't tell if a female or male was in the driver's seat. Maybe it was an official car from the Coast Guard.

After everyone had left, Brain asked Stephanie, "I would like to stay with you tonight, Steph."

"Brian, if you don't mind, I would like to spend the night alone in my apartment tonight. I'm really exhausted and need lots of sleep more than anything. I'll call you tomorrow."

"Do you think you are able to drive your car?"

"Yes, that I can do."

As Ramon and the lieutenant were walking back to their cars, "Lieutenant, so far, I haven't been able to locate Eva to bring her in for questioning."

Eva was a prime suspect especially with her reputation as a possible stalker of Brian.

"Let me know when you do. Put her in an interrogation room. One with a one-way mirror. I want to see and hear everything Ramon, so don't start without me."

"You've got it, Lieutenant."

The one-way mirror allowed officials to see and hear suspects being interrogated without them knowing it. They only saw their reflections in the mirror.

Ramon finally located Eva early that morning at her father's house.

"Eva, we need you to come down to the police station to answer a few questions."

Eva's father said, "What is this all about, Eva?"

"I have no idea, Daddy."

"Go with the detectives hon, and I will meet you down there."

He took her aside and said in a low voice, "Do not answer any questions until my lawyer is there."

"I understand, Daddy."

Eva's father called his lawyer the minute they left. Unfortunately, he was out of town and would not be back until Monday.

Ramon sat across from Eva and her father in the interrogation room. The lieutenant was on the other side of the one-way mirror. Listening to the proceedings.

"Eva, can you account for your whereabouts from 4:00 pm yesterday until this morning when you were at your father's house?"

Her father nodded his okay for her to answer.

"Of course. I was out of town visiting a good friend of mine. We joined some of our friends for an early dinner."

"How long were you at your friend's house?"

"I stayed overnight, then went to my fathers this morning."

"Can your friends validate all this?"

"Of course."

Ramon then covered all the details of Brian's boat drifting out to the ocean.

"Do you know anything about this, Eva?"

"No, I do not."

From then on every question Ramon asked was answered by, "I need to speak to my lawyer."

The lieutenant buzzed Ramon to excuse himself. Ramon stood up, "Excuse me, I will be back in a minute."

The lieutenant was standing next to a projector and was very excited about something. He told Ramon what had just happened. Ramon returned to the interrogation room.

"So, Eva, you are denying you had anything to do with this?"

"I need to speak to my lawyer before I answer any more of your questions."

"That is certainly your right. Perhaps, Eva, this will help improve your memory."

The door opened and a projector was wheeled into the room and turned on.

"Daddy, this is ridiculous."

"I know, sweetheart, I know."

When the screen lit up, a clear picture came into view of Eva untying the lines of Brian's boat and dropping them into the water. Eva paled and looked like she was going to faint. Brian's boat was the last one at the end of the dock and would easily drift out into the open ocean, especially with the help of the approaching storm and strong currents.

In shock, Eva's father said, "How could you have done this,

Eva?"

Ramon stood behind Eva and read her rights. Eva's father sat there in shock, completely devastated.

"Eva Peters, you are under arrest for attempted murder, please stand."

The jailor came in and cuffed Eva. Her father said, "Eva, I'll contact my lawyer right away," as the jailor led her out of the room.

Eva's father said to Ramon, "Detective, was anyone on that boat?"

"Yes, Mr. Peter's, one person."

"I hope they were not hurt."

"Fortunately, no, but it could have gone the other way very easily."

"Mr. Peters, I am so sorry. I know how you must feel. A private citizen and his wife loved Eva's boat and had made an unsuccessful offer to buy it from Eva. He went back to the marina to take pictures of the boat so they could find another one like it. After the pictures were developed and he saw the picture of Eva untying the boat lines on Brian's boat and then dropping them in the water, he knew something was wrong. He returned to the marina and gave the pictures to the proper authorities."

"Detective, would you do me a favor?"

He handed Ramon his card.

"Please tell this individual I no longer have any use for this boat and would like to transfer ownership to him and his wife."

"I understand, sir. I will contact him right away."

"Thank you, detective."

Eva's father certainly could withstand the loss of the $70,000 he paid for the boat for his daughter, but not the loss of his daughter. If he had only seen the other side of her, maybe this could have been prevented with the proper medical treatment. He could only pray they could use this in her defense. He would contact his lawyer immediately when he returned to his office on Monday.

CHAPTER 73

Ralph Barnes and his wife were having lunch. He was thinking about how glad he was that he had turned in that photograph to the marina manager. He would follow up on it later to see if anything came of it.

The phone rang, he answered it.

"Oh, hello Detective."

His wife noticed he looked very surprised.

"Are you sure Detective? That's very generous of Mr. Peter's. I will call him right away."

He hung up.

"What is it Ralph?"

"Honey, you're never going to believe this."

CHAPTER 74

The next day, Brian called his mom, Alecia.

"Mom, you won't believe what has happened."

"Oh no, not again."

"Can you and Jim meet me for Chinese tonight?"

"Is it bad news again, or do you just like Chinese food?"

"Well, I'll put it this way, it's bad news, ending in very good news."

Brain told her the whole story, Alecia said, "Brian, that is unbelievable! By the way, how is your relationship going with Stephanie?"

"It's a bit off."

"Well, you can't blame her, Brian. That was a terrifying experience."

CHAPTER 75

Later that day, Stephanie joined the lieutenant in his office with Ramon to discuss the case against Eva.

The lieutenant said, "Thank goodness, for those damaging pictures that individual inadvertently took. Now, if we can just prove Eva knew you were on that boat alone, Stephanie."

"Lieutenant, Eva did know. When I was boarding Brian's boat, Eva saw me and asked,

'Where's Brian?'

I told her he was still at USC and would be down later in a few hours, so Eva did know I was on the boat alone."

The lieutenant smiled at Ramon and Stephanie. He loved to quote the line from the popular T.V. show the "A" Team with his own modification.

"*I love it when a plan comes together*, especially a good prosecution one. How about a drink before we all go home?"

"Lieutenant, if you don't mind, I am exhausted and think I'll head for home."

"I understand Stephanie, I want you to take off one week to rest up."

"Thank you, Lieutenant."

CHAPTER 76

It seemed wonderful just to relax and not go to work the next day. She felt relieved she and Brian had decided to go their separate ways. But something was missing, it was Mitch. She just couldn't seem to get Mitch out of her mind. She had known Mitch was someone she would not be able to forget that easily, or not want to for that matter. She liked everything about him from the beginning. Even his name, she had noticed it emblazoned on his jacket when he dropped from the helicopter ladder onto the boat deck. Mitch Grant. It sounded nice and strong, just like him.

Stephanie and Mitch were so much alike in so many ways. They were both well-educated and were very skilled in their professions which were extremely dangerous. However, there was one area in which they were completely the opposite. Mitch was in the Coast Guard and loved the water, Stephanie liked to be on good old terra firma. She was uncomfortable and afraid of the water.

Stephanie's phone rang showing an unknown number. It was probably a solicitor. Without thinking she answered it.

"Hi pretty lady." Her heart started racing. It was Mitch.

"Mitch it's so good to hear your voice."

"Yours, too. I thought I'd try to catch you off guard at the last minute and take you to dinner tonight. Are you free?"

"As a matter of fact, I am."

"That's great. Why don't I come by your place about 6:30 pm. Be thinking of someplace special."

She gave him her apartment address.

"I can hardly wait to see you, Stephanie."

"I feel the same Mitch."

It seemed like it took forever to reach 6:30 pm until finally the doorbell rang. Right on time. Stephanie took a deep breath and tried to compose herself. The minute she opened the door Mitch reached for her and kissed her deeply.

"I could hardly wait to do that. I'm skipping formalities, pretty lady."

She felt like saying 'me too Mitch. Why don't we take off our clothes and go into my bedroom.' Instead she said, "Come in Mitch. I'll fix us drinks. What would you like?"

"Scotch and water sounds great. Can I help?"

"No. Make yourself comfortable." She pointed to the sofa. She noticed how great he looked in his sports clothes, so rugged and handsome. When he took off his jacket she could see his muscles standing out through his shirt. Stephanie brought over their drinks and placed them on the coffee table in front of the sofa. She sat next to him and they toasted each other.

"You know I've been very worried about you."

"And why is that?"

"I remember when we were on the boat and I asked you how you got there and you mentioned you thought someone was trying to do you in."

"Actually that was true."

"Can you tell me about it?"

"A little. Since then that person has been apprehended and is in custody awaiting trial for attempted murder. I can't tell you anymore because it's an ongoing investigation."

"Thank goodness you are safe now. My next question is are you still seeing that guy Brian what's his name?"

"No, I'm not."

"Anyone else?"

"Nope."

"Good. Where would you like to go to dinner tonight? Anyplace you like that's special?"

"I have an idea since we haven't seen each other for a while."

"Okay, shoot."

"Do you like Chinese?"

"I love it."

"I was thinking we could stay here at my place and order Chinese in. That would give us a chance to catch up on things. The place down the street has incredible Chinese food. What do you think?"

"That sounds great to me Stephanie."

"What do you like?"

"Everything."

"Is there anything you don't like?"

"I don't think so."

"Good. I'll order for us later. I'm going to refresh our drinks."

She added some tasty Chinese appetizers she had in the refrigerator.

"Mmm, these are really good."

"Let me know when you are hungry and I'll call in our order."

Mitch moved closer to her on the sofa and put his arm around her.

"You know you're all I've thought about since we've been back."

"I'm glad you called Mitch."

"By the way, I love your place."

"Thank you."

"It feels like you."

He kissed her lightly teasing her with his tongue then more deeply. They became more intimate and his hand moved downward to her breast, then went underneath her sweater. Stephanie moaned lightly, she could feel his hardness growing against her body.

"Stephanie I think we should go to your bedroom."

"I agree."

They couldn't take their clothes off fast enough as they went to her bedroom. As they fell into her bed they couldn't seem to get enough of each other.

"Mitch I want you now."

As he spread her legs, she could feel him start to enter her. He started thrusting in and out, their bodies moving together faster and faster. She cried out as her body started contracting with one orgasm after another. To heighten their climax he withdrew partially then thrust in again and again. This frenzy continued until they both cried out as they came to an explosive climax. They fell back on the bed in complete exhaustion.

"Wow, Mitch you are something else."

"So are you Stephanie."

"Mitch I think we've worked up an appetite. What do you think, should I order?"

"Absolutely."

The Chinese food was out of this world. They ate almost everything.

"This is the best Chinese food I've ever had. I'm glad you thought of it Steph."

"I also have a great Chinese liquor I think you will like."

"Mmm, this is really good."

"You know the Asians know a lot about what enhances sex. However, I don't think we need any more help in that area," Mitch laughed.

"I agree."

"I'm having such a great time with you. I don't want to leave."

"You don't have to, you can stay over, if you want."

"I was hoping you would ask me.

"By the way, do you have any time off work coming?"

"I do, a whole week."

"Me too."

"Would you like to go to wine country?"

"Which one?"

"I was thinking of Paso Robles."

"Let's do it."

"Do you need to call work?"

"No, I'm all set."

"Me too. On our way back we can take our time and stop at some of the beach cities, they have terrific jazz clubs. The music is outstanding and so is the seafood. This trip will be great."

"We can get an early start in the morning."

They looked at each other.

"Are you thinking what I'm thinking?"

"Maybe."

"Let's pack some things and leave right now. We won't have any traffic. We can be in Santa Barbera in no time and spend the night there."

"What will you do for clothes?"

Mitch looked very sheepish.

"I was hoping you would ask me to stay over so I put an assortment of clothes in the trunk of my car."

She smiled up at him, "Pretty confident, weren't you?"

"I could only hope."

With hardly any traffic, they reached Santa Barbera in no time.

They checked in at a very nice motel for the night. The motel had a restaurant where they could have breakfast before they took off for the wine country in the morning. Stephanie loved sleeping with Mitch. She slept on her side with his strong muscular arms wrapped around her.

The next morning they got off to an early start with a hearty breakfast at the motel where they were staying. They had done some research on the wineries and knew which ones they wanted to visit. They couldn't get over the breathtaking countryside. They were able to visit three (3) wineries a day and enjoy gourmet food during the day and evening at the local places. They took their time going home looking forward to going to well-known jazz clubs and sumptuous seafood.

The small towns of Redondo and Hermosa Beach were well known for musicians and singers who later became very famous. The music was always terrific, they could have stayed much longer. Unfortunately, *tempus fugit*, time flies, work was calling.

CHAPTER 77

Mario Rossi and Gino Bianchi were having dinner together in the San Quentin prison cafeteria. Mario had a bad reputation as a well known major crime boss. His record was about as long as his arm. He either liked you or he didn't. If he didn't like you, well, that was another story. But for some unknown reason, he and Gino seemed to get along.

"Just think Gino, you will be out of this hell-hole by tomorrow afternoon."

"I can hardly wait Mario."

"I have a job for you Gino, if you are interested."

"Tell me about it Mario."

"You remember that detective, Stephanie what's-her-name, the one that put me in here for murder for the rest of my life?"

"I do Mario, a real looker."

"That's the one."

"I would like to see her permanently taken care of."

"How much Mario?"

"20 big ones. $10,000 up front and $10,000 when you finish the job."

"What do you say?"

Gino sat there thinking. He had done some jobs like this before, luckily he had never been caught. He had only been in prison for the drugs. But it had still been a long 7 years. He knew he didn't have a dime when he walked out of prison tomorrow, and he knew that Mario was good for the money.

"I don't have all day Gino. Make up your mind."

"I'll do it. Do you have a picture of her?"

"I do." Mario handed him a newspaper clipping from his pocket.

"When you leave tomorrow, Gino, a black SUV will be outside the gate waiting for you. My business manager, Tom, will give you your first payment of $10,000 in cash. He will also give you his contact number for you to call when you complete the job and where to meet him to collect your final payment of $10,000."

CHAPTER 78

The following afternoon, Gino felt like a new man as he left prison. He spotted the black SUV waiting for him. When he got in, Mario's business manager Tom gave him a thick envelope with the $10,000 in cash. Gino counted it just to be sure it was all there. It was.

"I'm going into the next big city and can give you a lift if you need one."

"That would be great, Tom."

He also gave Gino another envelope with his contact number so when Gino completed the job, he would know where to meet him for his final payment of $10,000.

When Gino reached the next city, he decided to celebrate and splurge a little. He chose a four star hotel that had a great restaurant and bar. He checked in, took a long hot shower and changed into his good clothes. He went to the bar in search of a good drink and female companionship. There was an empty bar stool next to a very attractive lady. He took it and introduced himself.

"Hi, my name is Gino. May I buy you a drink?"

"Why, yes, you may. I'm Beth. That's very nice of

you."

They enjoyed each other's company over a few drinks.

"Would you like to join me for dinner?"

"Yes, I would."

They took their time enjoying talking to each other and the superb food.

"Beth, it's still early. Why don't we get to know each other better and have an after dinner drink in my room?"

She agreed.

Gino couldn't get over his luck, almost all his needs were being met, except sex, which they accomplished in no time.

CHAPTER 79

Gino didn't waste any time the next morning. He called the station in Northern California to make sure the detective was still there.

"Stephanie Green, homicide, please."

"I'm sorry, sir, but she's no longer at this location."

"Could you tell me where I could reach her?"

"She calls in frequently for her messages. Could I tell her who called?"

"No, thank you."

Gino started the painstaking process of calling all of the other stations in Northern California. He decided, after an unsuccessful search, he would try Southern California. Maybe she had relocated there.

"Stephanie Green, homicide, please."

Bingo.

"She's out of the office sir, could I take a message?"

"No, thank you. Do you know when she might

return?"

"No, sir, I don't."

"Thank you. I'll try later."

Gino caught the next flight to Southern California right away. He rented a car and checked in at a motel close to her station. He drove the area to become familiar with the surroundings. He saw an outdoor café across from the station which would be ideal for a stakeout. He was starving and decided now was as good a time as any to grab a bite. He was hungry and ordered a pastrami sandwich and an ice cold beer. He laid his newspaper and notepad on the table.

A couple of hours passed before he spotted her leaving the station. It was 5:30, she was probably on her way home. He wrote down her license plate, make and model of her car. He threw $20 on the table to cover his lunch and jumped in his car. He followed her to an apartment a few miles away. When she drove in her subterranean garage, he noticed there was no security. Perfect.

The next day, he returned to the outdoor café to learn more about her schedule. At noon, a handsome guy met her at the station's front door, probably to take her to lunch. They got in his car and Gino wrote down his license plate, make and model of the car.

Gino went to her apartment and drove thru her garage on a regular basis. He saw her boyfriend's car parked there frequently in the space next to hers. He stayed overnight frequently. This presented a temporary problem for Gino's sabotage plans for the detective.

Before his life of crime, Gino was an excellent mechanic. He decided to fix the detective's car brakes so they would fail immediately in a high speed chase. He would have to pick a time when her boyfriend's car was not in the garage.

The next day, Gino hadn't seen the detective go into the station early in the morning. Out of curiosity, he called.

"Stephanie Green, please."

"No, I'm sorry. Detective Green will be out of the office for the next few days."

Gino thought, 'How lucky can I get? I should be able to wrap this up in no time.'

Gino checked her garage to see if she had left her car there. She had.

Gino left at 2:00 am that morning for her apartment. He drove in her garage and parked his car in the vacant spot next to hers, where her boyfriend parked. He took out his mechanics tool kit and got to work. It didn't take long for him to fix her breaks the way he wanted to. They would be passable until she had to step on them really hard to avoid a terrible accident. He made sure he picked up the mess he had made. He left satisfied with his work.

CHAPTER 80

Gino saw a bulletin board notice in his hotel for the Catalina Express boat schedule. He always loved Catalina and decided to go there for a few days. It would also give him a good alibi.

He checked in at a relatively inexpensive hotel when he got there and changed into comfortable beach wear. He took a large beach towel from the hotel in case he wanted to lie in the sand and sunbathe after breakfast. He ended up sunbathing all afternoon. 'This is the life,' he thought.

He chose a nice restaurant for dinner. The bar was packed so with a martini, he decided to have dinner first and try his luck at the bar later. While he was eating his dinner, something caught his eye at a nearby table across the room. Oh my god, it looked like the detective and her boyfriend. He heard the boyfriend call her Stephanie a few times. He put his plan in motion. He would stay in Catalina after they returned to the mainland. He would call her office periodically until they told him about her fatal accident.

Gino waited several days and called the station. She had returned, but there was no word of any accident. He was beginning to worry. It had been a long time since he was a mechanic, maybe he forgot something. He might have to return to the mainland and recheck her brakes.

His phone rang. It was Mario.

"Gino, how's everything going? Any news yet?"

Gino started sweating, "The plan is in motion, Mario."

"Don't disappoint me Gino."

CHAPTER 81

"Mitch, I have an early morning meeting tomorrow, enjoy your day off."

"Ok, hon."

When Mitch got in his car the next morning, something caught his eye in Stephanie's empty space as he was backing out. Curious, he got out of his car to see what it was. It looked like a piece of machinery from her car. He didn't like the looks of it and took it to Harry, the car mechanic at Stephanie's station. He called Stephanie and told her what he had found.

"Since I've got the day off, I am going to wait while Harry checks it."

"Okay, let me know when I can drive my car."

"Harry. Could you do me a favor?"

"Sure, Mitch. What is it?"

He handed him what he had found.

"What do you think this is?"

"Looks like something from a car's breaking system."

"Can you check Stephanie's car? I think her car may have been tampered with."

"Sure thing. Right away."

"I'll wait. Thank you Harry."

"Well Mitch, I'm glad you brought Stephanie's car in. You're right, somebody has been tampering with her car. The breaks would have failed completely in any high speed chase. I'll put some new ones in for her."

"Thanks, Harry. I'll let her know."

"Well, pretty lady. Somebody's after you again."

"What was it, Mitch?"

"Your breaks. They would have failed if you had pushed hard on them. Harry put in new ones for you."

Gino called Stephanie's station from Catalina to see if she had returned to work. She had. He waited a few more days, then called again. No fatalities reported. He was getting worried, maybe he forgot something when he fixed her brakes, after all, it had been a few years since he was a car mechanic. He decided to return to the mainland and recheck them.

"What are you thinking, Steph?"

"The best way to catch this guy. I'll put my car back in my apartment space, and I'll use another car when I'm in the field. I'll stay with you at your place. I like the idea that you cannot enter your subterranean garage unless you have a code to enter."

"What are your plans to catch this guy?"

"I'll have an alarm system installed and I'll put two undercover officers in the garage 24/7. I think whoever did this will come back to check the brakes to see if he forgot something and the alarm will go off. The undercover guys will be waiting for him."

"I like it."

"Good."

Stephanie put her car back in her garage right away. Gino drove by her apartment and saw her car in the garage. Gino assumed she hadn't driven it. He would recheck her brakes again that evening if her boyfriend wasn't there.

Around 3:00 am, the alarm went off in a loud shrill.

CHAPTER 82

The undercover officers drew their guns and caught Gino off guard. They arrested him, read him his rights, gathered his tool kit and supplies for evidence, and took him to the station charging him with attempted murder.

CHAPTER 83

The station was unusually busy that day. Gino was told to sit down until his name was called to be processed.

Gino asked the guard, "May I use the restroom?"

The guard nodded his okay.

When Gino started to leave the restroom, he heard lots of noise and shouting coming from outside the door. He opened it slowly and saw a large group of noisy protesters were being brought into the station. They were shouting and were completely out of control. The guards had arrested them for causing all kinds of unlawful trouble to the city and its citizens.

In all the commotion and confusion, Gino walked out of the restroom, through the crowd of protesters, and out of the station completely unnoticed. He remembered a bus depot being close by and started walking as fast as he could. Maybe he could catch the next bus out of town before they discovered he was missing.

He bought a ticket for the next bus which was leaving for Texas. In the convenience store, he bought a hat which covered half of his face, and a long-sleeved shirt to cover his tattoos. He disposed of his current t-shirt in the bus station restroom and replaced it with his new shirt. He got in line to board the bus and saw a lady by herself and pretended that they were together.

CHAPTER 84

Stephanie was in her office when her phone buzzed, it was the lieutenant.

"Stephanie, we have a problem."

He told her what had just happened.

"How long ago did he walk out, lieutenant?"

"About 10 minutes ago."

"Ok, he may have tried to make a run for the bus depot a few blocks away. I'm going there now. Do we have a picture of him?"

"Yes, at the front desk."

"I'll pick that up on the way out."

"Good. All major departure locations have received a warrant for his arrest."

Stephanie threw on a coat to cover her uniform and put on a wig she kept in her office for situations like these. She picked up Gino's picture at the front desk as she flew out the door and left in an undercover car.

When she reached the bus depot she saw a line of people waiting to board the next bus. She noticed it was going to Texas. She scanned the group in line but didn't see anyone suspicious. When they were all on board and seated, she showed the bus driver her badge and told him to wait a few minutes before leaving.

She walked down the aisle looking carefully at the passengers. She came to a couple with a man wearing a hat that partially covered his face. She heard the woman talking to him and he kept on nodding his head, but not talking. When she got closer, she realized the woman was speaking in a foreign language and he just kept nodding like he understood.

Gino started sweating again.

She showed him her badge, "Sir, please remove your hat and stand up. Gino Bianchi, you are under arrest."

She cuffed him and read him his rights. Stephanie took Gino in the station to be processed.

An officer was at the front desk, "Thank you, Stephanie. Sorry about everything. We'll take it from here."

"I'll wait here until the jailer takes him to his cell. He can be a little slippery."

Afterwards, Stephanie went in the lieutenants office.

"Steph, bring me up to date with Gino Bianchi. I still can't believe he walked right thru those protestors and out of our station. Where is he now?"

"In one of our jail cells. I caught him at the bus station and he's been processed and is sitting in a jail cell."

"Good work."

"I also know who put out the contract on me lieutenant."

"Who was it?"

"Gino's friend at San Quentin, Mario Rossi."

"Wasn't that the one you put in San Quentin for life on that murder charge?"

"Yes, it was."

"Stephanie, you know *I love it when a plan comes together*, and yours always seem to."

"Why, thank you, lieutenant."

CHAPTER 85

"Well, pretty lady. It's time for me to leave for my Coast Guard assignment. I'll probably be gone for a few days. I'll call you the minute it's over."

"You better. I'll miss you."

Mitch grabbed her, hugged her tightly and kissed her, "I'll miss you too. Do we have time for a quickie?"

"Are you crazy, Mitch? Our quickies are never quick."

"I want you bad, pretty lady."

"Oh, for pete's sake, Mitch. You know I can't resist you."

CHAPTER 86

The Coast Guard had been suspicious of a large yacht coming in from Mexico. It was several miles out in the ocean. They decided to examine their cargo before the yacht decided to divert to another location. They surrounded the yacht with another Coast Guard vessel and went aboard to examine the cargo. They finally discovered the cargo they were looking for. They towed the yacht into the Catalina harbor and offloaded one of the largest drug busts of cocaine and marijuana.

Mitch could hardly wait to tell Stephanie. He was proud to have played a major part in the capture of the drugs and offenders. It gave him a good feeling to know that the drugs and offenders would never cause harm to anyone.

He texted Stephanie right away about their success,

"Just wrapping up everything now. Should be done in an hour or two."

She texted him back,

"You're in all the newspapers and TV. LET'S CELEBRATE!! I'm taking the late afternoon Catalina plane over. Will meet you at your hotel at 5:00 pm.

I'm sure we can think of something to do before dinner."

ACKNOWLEDGEMENTS

Erin Wolfe, my outstanding computer guru, who does a wonderful job of deciphering my handwriting and entering it into the computer perfectly.

My good friend, Susie Tatum, aka "The Proofer," who always does a terrific job of proofreading and critiquing my books.

My good friend, Doris Potter, who did an outstanding job of editing my book.

A special thanks to my good friends for all of their help and support. Carolyn Rudell, for her boating expertise, Chris Madlem, Claudia Morrett, Helen Wilkes, Tom Jones, and Toni Joseph, for her outstanding research.

Thank you to my good friend Joseph Caro for my book cover.

And a very big thank you to all my wonderful friends and readers who encourage me every day to keep writing.

Made in the USA
Middletown, DE
01 February 2022

60215823R00161